MYHAT IN EGYPT

THROUGH THE EYES OF A GOD

BY

ALUN BUFFRY

ADULT FICTION

MYHAT IN EGYPT
THROUGH THE EYES OF A GOD

BY

ALUN BUFFRY

Published by ABeFree Publishing: 2016
ISBN 978-0-9932107-7-8

Disclaimer:

This is a work of fiction. Names, characters, places and incidents either are products of the author's imagination or are used fictitiously. Any resemblance to actual events or locales or persons, living or dead, is entirely coincidental.

Acknowledgements and Accreditations

With thanks to Matt Maguire <info@candescentpress.co.uk>
Thanks to Lesley James for the photograph of the author.

.

Thanks to Melissa Dawson for helping with the text.

Elements of the cover were adapted from photographs by Dennis Jarvis and CDDinosaur
shared under a Creative Commons license (CC BY-SA 2.0)

In loving memory of Susan Beswick.

CONTENT

BY THE SAME AUTHOR

FROM DOT TO CLEOPATRA, A CONCISE HISTORY OF
ANCIENT EGYPT
ISBN 1-872914-09-8 (Frontier Publishing, Windetts, Kirstead,
Norfolk, NR15 1BR, UK)
http://buffry.org.uk/fromdot.html

DAMAGE AND HUMANITY IN CUSTODY
ISBN 978-0-9932107-0-9 (ABeFree Publishing)

OUT OF JOINT - 20 YEARS OF CAMPAIGNING FOR
CANNABIS
ISBN 978-1-5084202-1-7 (ABeFree Publishing)
http://www.buffry.org.uk/outofjoint.html

ALL ABOUT MY HAT - THE HIPPY TRAIL 1972
ISBN 978-0-9932107-1-6 (ABeFree Publishing)
http://www.buffry.org.uk/allaboutmyhat.html

TIME FOR CANNABIS: THE PRISON YEARS
ISBN 978-0-8832107-6-1
ABeFree Publishing http://www.buffry.org.uk/timeforcannabis.html

all available at AMAZON and through good bookshops.

INTRODUCTION BY MYHAT

Before I tell you my incredible story of my journeys to Egypt with Ed, I must explain that I am a hat!

My first memories were from the early 1970's, although I know I am older than that. In those days, I spent a great amount of time hanging on a hook in a barber's shop in Thessaloniki in Greece and from there I had a very limited experience and concept of the world. The barber's name was Konstantinos and sometimes he used to take me off my hook and put me on his head; then I could experience more.

Let me tell you a little about myself.

You see I am no ordinary hat. I am able to see, hear, smell and even taste through the senses of the person wearing me. In fact, I can often pick up on their thoughts, memories, dreams and even fears.

But, from that hook, I mostly witnessed conversations between Konstantinos and his customers, whilst he cut their hair or shaved their beards, which for me seemed to be a strange thing to do at that time. Their talk was about the weather, the people that ran their lives and a game called football.

Konstantinos used to say to his customers some words I always remembered and heeded: watch, listen and remember! That is how I came to write my books.

It was on a sunny day in early 1972 that my life was to change drastically and mostly for the better, for on that day whilst Konstantinos was standing in his doorway, there being no customers, and with me on his head, we spotted a small group of young people walking down the dusty street. Konstantinos called over a young man and presented me to him, saying "You have no hat. Here, take Myhat."

That is how I come to know my name as Myhat as before that I was called Kapelomou.   My new head was called "Al".

Al was travelling eastwards with his small group of friends and eastwards we went, through countries called Turkey, Syria, Iraq, Iran, Afghanistan, Pakistan and India.   Before that all I knew as my world was the barber's shop and the street outside.   Now I was travelling the world.   That is my other story: 'All About Myhat: The Hippy Trail 1972'.

In 1989, I found myself upon the head of Ed, after Al left me behind one day, and I travelled with Ed for over twenty years until, one day, he gave me back to Al.

When Al started wearing me more often again, I was able to somehow get through to him and write my accounts of our times together in 1972 and my times in Egypt with Ed and Ana.   That is how I came to write this history.

It took several years of trying before I managed to plant the idea of writing books into Al's head and even as I write this today, he seems unaware that I am, in fact, a sentient being myself.   Al thinks it was all his idea!   Most disappointing, yet even when I gave him the idea that I, Myhat, was the true author, when he mentioned it to his friends they seemed to think he was crazy!

The main thing of course is that I managed to get my story published.

One day, in 1989, I met Ed.   Al had left me at Ed's house and Ed started wearing me a lot.

Ed and Ana and myself visited Egypt in 1989, 1990 and again in 2010 and this is the incredible tale of those journeys and what happened to us, on our travels through space and time.

In ancient Egypt the name Ana name meant Goddess.

I did spend time also on Ana's head too.

By 1989, Ana had studied many languages. By 2010 she could speak Arabic and read some Hieroglyphs.

It seems strange to me that almost every country we visited had its own languages and often its own religions, politics and lifestyles; people had their own individual dreams and fears and even their own ideas and beliefs about what would happen after their bodies died and were disposed of in their various ways. I often wonder what will happen to me too. For me, my life has meant being passed round various heads.

I have experienced much more than anyone, I think, could anticipate.

Now I know that I am a God, much more than a hat, for I have seen the world through the eyes of a God.

Let me tell you how that came to be.

OUT OF MY BOX

Ed was planning to visit a country called Egypt for the first time, with a girl called Ana, who was younger than him. Ed was twenty-nine years of age.

Ed had met a great number of interesting people with fascinating ideas and one of the issues raised in his mind was about the Great Pyramid just outside Cairo. It was said to have been built almost 5000 years earlier, during the reign of a Pharaoh called *Cheops* or *Khufu*.

Ed, however, was not entirely convinced that a structure of that size and accurate construction could have been built in the so-called Stone Age.

Ed had calculated that this one Great Pyramid alone contained millions of heavy stones, placed with great accuracy and aligned to the poles, and that placement of stones would have to be done at the rate of more than one per minute almost non-stop if the task was to be completed in 20 years as the books claimed.

They would need to cut the stones and transport and lift them, some to hundreds of feet in the air, to be placed accurately by a people that did not even know about wheels and pulleys.

Moreover, galleries, chambers and corridors had to be built-in.

Apparently, nobody actually knew how the building was done.

Even with modern technology, Ed had read, no construction company in the world would take on such a project.

Neither did anybody know why the pyramids had been built at all.

Some say that the pyramids had been used as tombs, yet no

body had been found within, just a large but empty stone sarcophagus with a broken lid.

Others said the pyramid served as an initiation chamber. But, Ed thought, there were actually three massive pyramids on the same plain at Giza, just outside Cairo. Why would they need three initiation chambers?

Others believed they were built in a way that represented the appearance in the sky of the constellation of Orion, known in ancient Egypt as *Osiris*, or at least his "belt", possibly, they said, by an unknown race on earth who wanted to send us a message.

Ed had concluded, there was not even any proof of when they had been built.

Ed had also read books that claimed that even small pyramids had strange properties; even when made from cardboard or wood, the shape was said to be able to sharpen razor blades, purify water and even heal illnesses.

Ed was determined to find out more about the Great Pyramid and hence planned to visit Egypt in 1989 with Ana, to spend a week in Cairo and a week in Luxor.

This is where our adventure was to start, yet it was to last another twenty years before it came to an end.

1989 CAIRO

I went to Egypt with Ed and Ana in February to coincide with Ed's birthday. We flew from London, going from the cold weather to delightfully warm. We landed at Cairo airport and, as Ed and Ana already had their visas, we passed quickly through immigration and customs formalities and went to the bank to change some money. We were changing UK Pounds to Egyptian pounds at the rate of about one to four. Ed smiled as he approached everyone as he had been told that was the key in Egypt and he certainly received smiles back.

"Do you like trips?" asked the teller at the bank kiosk, smiling broadly.

For a moment. Ed wondered if they were about to be offered LSD. Surely not at a bank in Cairo Airport, he thought. It was then that he spotted a couple of bottles of fizzy drink, called '*Tripps*'.

"Yes we do", Ed said and he and Ana were promptly passed two bottles that were opened by the desk teller. They drank the *Tripps*, changed their money, waved goodbye and set of to find the pre-arranged shuttle bus to the Hotel Sheraton, a Five Star, in the city centre.

Ana was an attractive and intelligent lady, a couple of years younger than Ed. Ana had studied and graduated in languages at the same university of East Anglia as Ed had attended studying chemistry. Ed was very fond of Ana.

Ed and Ana spent 7 nights in Cairo, visiting the many sites, realising there was much more in Egypt than the Pyramids to fascinate them.

They would be visiting the Giza plateau pyramids and Sphinx and the pyramids at Saqqara.

Their first visit to see The Great Pyramid was on their second day in Cairo and they went by taxi. As soon as they had arrived and descended from the Shuttle bus from the airport, they had been approached (almost accosted) by a taxi driver who promised to be there waiting at their convenience and, sure enough, he was there that morning to take them through the noisy heavy traffic to Giza, to show them where to go, give them advice, and wait there for them whenever they chose to move on.

Ed thought it was a good move to have a personal taxi available and the price was very cheap. As if it had been his idea!

 Ed and Ana approached the Great Pyramid of Cheops. It was totally massive. They were amazed and pleased to see that today it was open to the public.

They had to buy tickets and them climb up to an entrance that had previously been blown open with dynamite; it was not the original entrance. Inside they had to climb up and down wooden ramps as they moved towards the Grand Gallery and then the Kings Chamber.

It was unbelievably large; I know Ed and Ana were somewhat mesmerized. I just concentrated on staying on Ed's head as he had to bow down as he moved inside the entrance and along the ramps. Those ancient Egyptians must have been small! I certainly did not want to fall down a shaft in here. It could be thousands of years again before I was found.

The King's Chamber, which Ed knew was not actually a king's chamber at all, being named as such in relatively modern times, was spacious. It was made of huge stone blocks, cut and placed to precision without mortar, so that even a small plastic credit card would not fit between. Above them was a massive stone roof; who knows how much weight ready to maybe fall on and squash us for ever. In the wall Ed could see a small square shaft entry that was once believed to have been for air circulating in ancient times although no exit shaft had been found outside. There was also the large granite sarcophagus with its broken lid on top, which again must have weighed tons. Ed had read that it was actually too big to get through the doorway so had been built in, presumably.

Ed and Ana stood alone in the Chamber (being unaware, as they were, that I was actually with them). They stood in silence. A great silence and stillness. It felt neither hot nor cold. Ed wondered again why this had been built and then sealed up. What had it been used for? How could anyone know the age when it was built, after all, dating stone is not the same as dating a building made of stone, for stones are many millions of years old and buildings only thousands. I wondered how anyone could even talk about millions of years.

Suddenly there was a great commotion from just outside the doorway. A crowd of tourists were filing into the Chamber. They were all chatting and laughing loudly; Ed recognised their language as French. One man stepped to the front and shouted "Ce n'est rien. Ce n'est rien. C'est vide".

I felt Ed react negatively to that, which he understood to mean "There's nothing, It's empty".

Ed did not said nothing aloud, but whispered in Ana's ear, "He's forgotten himself".

Ed and Ana left the Chamber and headed back outside, first visiting the Queens Chamber which was equally incredible to have been built.

Back outside, Ed and Ana sat for a while at the base of the pyramid enjoying the sun again. Ed was pondering out loud.

"I think it's really hard to comprehend the size of this pyramid, just that it's massive. When we come down from the road we couldn't even see anyone here, now we can't really see the real height because it slopes away from us. But this first level is almost as tall as us, each stone must weight tons. And how on earth did they build in those chambers and corridors?"

It was just then that an elderly Arabian-looking man in robes and sunglasses approached them with a beaming smile on his face and clutching a staff that looked like a wooden shepherd's crook with an animal head.

"My friends, my friends, welcome to Egypt. Welcome to pyramids. My name is Moses and I can tell you all information and show you good places."

Ed smiled and held out his hand, which Moses shook firmly. "Hello, my name is Ed."

"Greetings and welcome my good friend," said Moses, turning to Ana, "And this your Queen?"

"Yes," said Ed, knowing that it is so often better just to say that they were a couple or even married, in many countries and cultures. "This is Ana."

Ana held out her hand and Moses lowered his forehead to touch it, instead of shaking it.

"You like me to tell you about pyramid? Very big, yes. I tell you about it." Moses hardly paused before he delivered what must have been a well-practised speech.

"This is pyramid of Khufu and they say built by many men in twenty years. About 4500 years ago.

"Size is 420 feet and each side is 755 each long altogether over half mile to walk around, but not legal to climb up only OK for entrance and very dangerous to climb."

Ed felt as if Moses had read his mind as he had just been thinking of climbing. Ed had had done rock- climbing and walking up mountains in the UK whilst at University but then he had been twenty years old. Now he was less flt.

Moses carried on: "Inside pyramid Khufu is two and half

million stones, my friends. Inside will fit big Cathedral St Paul in London, also the Cathedrals of Rome, Florence, Milan and Westminster Abbey. Base of pyramid here like seven blocks in New York.

"Big Grand Gallery is 28 feet high and slope is 26 degrees and long is 157 feet.

"King's Chamber is 34 feet and 17 feet and height is 19 feet and big sarcophagus inside

"Queen's Chamber is little smaller."

"You want to go inside?", asked Moses.

"No, we have already been thanks," said Ed.

"OK I show you around? You want to walk around? It will take maybe thirty minutes, take your time. You have water? You go that way and walk to boat museum and I will wait for you there, show you museum, explain all to you, and show you special tomb if you want to go, not public, only for you to because I know you are good people. You are guests of Moses now!"

Ed and Ana did indeed have bottles of water as it was like a desert here and very hot and they agreed to meet Moses at the boat museum. Ed told Ana he was wondering what sort of boat would be in the desert.

The walk, as we had been told, was about half a mile but it was hot and sandy and they took their time, arriving after about half an hour at a building where they met again with Moses. He greeted them like old friends and took them to the entrance to the building that he said was "big boat museum".

Once inside the structure, Ed and Ana approached the boat. It was rather disappointing. Ed thought it was much larger. This one was impressive but Ed realised it would not actually carry anyone, But then again, he thought, it is no doubt symbolic.

Moses was standing next to them.

"You like?" he asked.

"Now you see real boat!"

Moses pointed upwards above their heads, and as Ed looked up, he realised they were actually standing under just the front section of the actual wooden boat itself; they had been looking at a model.

"This one of two Khufu ships," he said.

"This one built over 4500 years ago and put in ground in pieces. Now they put together again. It is hundred forty-three feet long and almost twenty feet wide. discovered in your 1954 by Kamal el-Mallakh. But this boat no sails so people say it was never on the water. It is with much Cedar wood from Leban. Now you go upstairs for good seeing, my friends, I tell you well."

Ed and Ana climbed the stairs and were totally impressed, I knew, by the wooden boat, lit by natural light through the roof. They were able to walk around it.

Back outside, Moses still talking and leading the way, waving his staff in the air and greeting everyone they passed, we headed towards the second largest pyramid, said to have been built a few years later for the Pharaoh Khafre.

"This little smaller pyramid," explained Moses, pointing.

"This one sides 706 feet and height is 448 feet. Also there were boats in ground but no longer there my friends. Khafre was son of Pharaoh Khufu. But Pyramid closed now for tourists."

A quick look outside and Moses suggested they visit "Tomb of Doctor". He led them back round the pyramid and a little way from it where sat a man. Moses spoke briefly to the man and said "You give him little baksheesh and he let you go down inside very beautiful my friend."

Ed knew that *baksheesh* was basically a bribe or reward for services and was the custom in many Asian countries. I had realised that although the smile and eye contact was the key to the meeting with most people, baksheesh was the way to get what you wanted and to say thanks. He had already been told to give just a few coins often, such as to the room cleaners at the hotel; just a few coins every day.

Ed had experience with caving, so when he saw the ladder going down just inside the doorway opened by the keeper with his large key, he was not perturbed.

"It's OK," he said to Ana; "I'll go first and you come down after me so you can't fall."

But it was very dark. The Keeper gave them a small plastic torch and Ed started descending into the black pit with Ana hesitantly above him, also descending.

They went down what must have been thirty steps on the ladder before Ed switched on the torch as the daylight from above was fading. The batteries were almost dead, they could see nothing. Ana wasn't happy even though Ed pointed the torch upwards for her.

"I don't like this," she said, "I can't see a thing. I want to go back up. It's too scary and anyway we won't be able to see what's down there if there's no lights."

Ed agreed. What was the point of climbing down who knew how far in darkness to see nothing and then have to climb up again? I knew too that he was concerned just in case they were locked in. Nobody other than the Keeper and Moses even knew they were there, and they hardly knew Moses anyway. What they were doing was probably illegal too. So he agreed and they both climbed up. Ed gave the torch back saying it was no good and needed new batteries, they could see nothing.

The Keeper just smiled. Moses said, "OK, now we have

camel ride then see Great Sphinx.

Ana and Ed did climb aboard a camel. Ed had ridden a camel in Rajasthan years earlier, that time along with a camel driver to keep control, for three days in that Indian desert. That had been an escorted ride but this was just a tourist gimmick. Ana held onto Ed tightly, she did not seem comfortable, whilst the tradesman took a few photos. They soon descended, then the tradesman gave Ed his thick djellaba to put on and persuaded Ed to climb up again, for more photos. When they descended, they had to pay, an amount Ed thought far too much, but he remembered the golden rule that he had forgotten: to always ask the price first, before getting into a taxi or even on to a camel. So he just paid. They visited the Sphinx complex, with the great stone beast itself dominating the view of the Pyramids in the background, and it's temples.

Moses related some information about the Sphinx which I knew Ed hardly heeded, being overcome somewhat by the view. I listened and remembered though. That is, after all, something I was very good at.

"Father of Fear," said Moses.

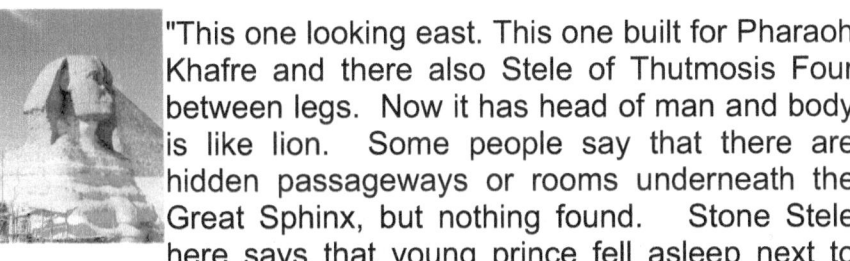"This one looking east. This one built for Pharaoh Khafre and there also Stele of Thutmosis Four between legs. Now it has head of man and body is like lion. Some people say that there are hidden passageways or rooms underneath the Great Sphinx, but nothing found. Stone Stele here says that young prince fell asleep next to the Sphinx, after hunting all day and very tired. In dream Great Sphinx promised prince can be powerful king of Upper and Lower Egypt after cleared the sand over up to neck. When Thutmosis older, he became great leader.

"This Sphinx is 240 feet long and 66 feet height and not built like pyramids; this one carved in rock."

Ed and Ana said goodbye to Moses and handed him some money. They went back to their taxi and told the driver to take them to Saqqara to see the Step Pyramids.

The step pyramid of King *Djoser*, which Ed pronounced as Hoser, was said to have pre-dated those at Giza.

Ed had an information brochure that explained that the *Hosar* pyramid was built under the design of a Royal Architect called *Imhotep* in the Third Dynasty in the 27th century BC. It said that previously people of renown or wealth were buried in pits in the ground, but that some were covered by a sort of stone bench that the Arabs called a mastaba. There were other kings that had pyramids built on the site at Saqqara but many were in a bad state and badly needed restoration.

Ed read aloud:

"The Pyramid *was built for the burial of Pharaoh Hoser by Imhotep, his vizier. It is the central feature of a vast mortuary complex in an enormous courtyard surrounded by ceremonial structures and decoration.*

"*This first Egyptian pyramid consisted of six mastabas of decreasing size built atop one another in what were clearly revisions and developments of the original plan. The pyramid originally stood 62 metres or 203 feet tall, with a base of 109 metres by 125 meters or 358 feet by 410 feet and was clad in polished white limestone.*"

"*Hoser was the first or second king of the 3rd Dynasty from about 2667 to 2648 BC and of the Old Kingdom. He is believed to have ruled for nineteen years or, if the nineteen years were biennial taxation years, thirty-eight years. He reigned long enough to allow the grandiose plan for his pyramid to be realised in his lifetime.*

"*Hoser is best known for his innovative tomb, which dominates the Saqqara landscape. In this tomb he is referred to by his Horus name Netjerykhet; Hoser is a name given by New Kingdom visitors thousands of years later. Hoser's step pyramid is astounding in its departure from previous architecture. It sets several important precedents, perhaps the most important of which is its status as the first monumental structure made of stone. The social implications of such a large and carefully sculpted stone structure are staggering. The process of building such a structure would be far more labour-intensive than previous monuments of mud-brick. This suggests that the state, and therefore the royal government had a new level of control of resources, both material and human. From this point on, kings of the Old Kingdom are buried in the North, rather than at Abydos. Furthermore, although the plan of Hoser's pyramid complex is different than later complexes, many elements persist and the step pyramid sets the stage for later pyramids of the fourth, fifth, and sixth dynasties, including the great pyramids at Giza. Finally, another intriguing first is the identification of the architect Imhotep, who is credited with the design and construction of the complex.*

"*The burial chamber is a vault constructed of four courses of well-dressed granite. It had one opening, which was sealed with a three-and-a-half ton block after the burial. No body was recovered as the tomb had been extensively robbed.*"

Ed said that he found it an impressive site and Ana agreed. It seemed very different to the Great Pyramid, somehow more feasible, she said. They chatted about how there was so much more to see in Egypt than they had thought and that the history itself was a longer period of time since the time of the Romans til now. In fact, Ana said, she knew that the ancient Romans had been in Egypt because of the tales of Caesar and Antony and Cleopatra. Ed wondered whether they had walked here. This place, he thought, would already have been ancient history for Cleopatra. In fact, prehistory, he thought.

The other pyramid close by was that of the Pharaoh Unas.

Ed read from the pamphlet: "The *Unas Pyramid is the smallest of the royal pyramids completed during the Old Kingdom. The accompanying mortuary complex with its high and valley temples linked by a 2,460 foot -long causeway was lavishly decorated with painted relief, whose quality and variety surpass the usual royal iconography.*

"Unas was the first Pharaoh to have the Pyramid texts carved and painted on the walls of the chambers of his pyramid. This, a major innovation that was followed by his successors until the First Intermediate Period, about 2160 BC. These texts identify the king with Ra and with Osiris, whose cult was on the rise in Unas' time, and were meant to help the king reach the afterlife.

"The pyramid lies between the pyramid of Sekhemkhet and the south western corner of the pyramid complex of Hoser, in symmetry with the pyramid of Userkaf located at the north eastern corner.

"The original Egyptian name of the pyramid was "Nefer Isut Unas", meaning "Beautiful are the places of Unas.

The main innovation of the pyramid of Unas is the first appearance of the Pyramid Texts, one of the oldest religious texts in Egypt to have survived to this day. In doing so, By including those Texts, Unas initiated a tradition that would be followed in the pyramid of the kings and queens of the Sixth to Eighth Dynasties, until the end of the Old Kingdom about two hundred years later.

"In total two hundred and eighty-three magical spells, also known as utterances, were carved and the signs painted in blue on the walls of the corridor, antechamber, and burial chamber of Unas' pyramid. They constitute the most complete rendition of the Pyramid Texts existing today. These spells were intended to help the king in overcoming hostile forces and powers in the Underworld and thus join with the sun god Ra, his divine father in the afterlife. By writing the texts on the walls of the pyramid's internal chambers, the architects of Unas' pyramid ensured that the king would benefit from their potency even if the funerary cult was to cease. Hence, the Pyramid Texts of the pyramid of Unas incorporate instructions for ritual actions and words to be spoken, suggesting that they were precisely those performed and recited during the cult of the king in his mortuary temple.

"The good preservation of the texts in Unas' pyramid shows

that they were arranged so as to be read by the Ba of Unas, as it arose from the sarcophagus thanks to resurrection utterances and surrounded by protective spells and ritual offerings. The Ba would then leave the burial chamber, which incorporates texts identifying the king with Osiris in the Duat, and would move to the antechamber symbolizing the Akhet. Included in the spells written on the walls of the antechamber of Unas are two utterances that belong to the 'Cannibal Hymn', which portrays the Pharaoh as flying to heaven through a stormy sky and eating both gods and men. In doing so the king would receive the life force of the gods. At this point the Ba of Unas would face east, the direction of the sunrise, and beyond the pyramid masonry, the false door of the mortuary temple where funerary rituals were performed. Finally, turning left the Ba would join Ra in the sky by passing through the pyramid corridor.

"*An example of spell from the pyramid of Unas is Utterance 217:*

Re-Atum, this Unas comes to you
A spirit indestructible
Your son comes to you
This Unas comes to you
May you cross the sky united in the dark
May you rise in light land, the place in which you shine!"

There was plenty of other stuff to see at Saqqara, but Ed and Ana were both tired and overwhelmed, so took their taxi back to the hotel.

Early that evening, Ana told Ed that she was going to the hotel's hairdresser. I felt that Ed had reservations and in fact he said to Ana "Are you sure? You could end up looking like an Egyptian movie-star." Ana laughed.

Ed dozed on the bed for the hour or more that Ana was away and woke up to see her standing in front on the bedroom mirror, combing her hair.

"You were right," she said, "look at me, I just wanted it trimmed but they did some style and set it and now it looks horrid. I'm going to have to wear a hat all the time. I can't go down for dinner looking like this."

"True," said Ed, "they'll all be lining up for your autograph!"

The following day, Ana and Ed spent hours in the Egyptian National Museum in Tahrir Square, within walking distance of the hotel. Ed took me off his head and put me into his bag whilst we were inside. I could still pick up on some of what he saw. Ana had undone the styling of her hair and was now happier about it.

Inside the museum, I felt that once again Ed and Ana were both amazed and overwhelmed by the amount to see on several floors. There were tall statues, large and small stone carvings, sarcophagi with and without mummies, mummified animals, scrolls, sections and furniture from tombs, temples and palaces.

"You know," Sid Ed, "there are plenty of books and pamphlets but there isn't one I've seen yet that makes any sense or order out of all this, they either skim over it or focus on just one or two bits."

"Well you ought to write one," said Ana.

The museum consisted of two floors. On the ground floor there were collections of papyrus and ancient coins, as well as a lot of artefacts from the New Kingdom, the time period between 1550 and 1069 BC.

On the first floor there were artefacts from the New Kingdom dynasties of Egypt, including items from the tombs of the Pharaohs Thutmosis the third and fourth. There were many artefacts from the Valley of the Kings and especially contents from the intact tombs of *Tutankhamun* and *Psuesennes* the first. Ed pronounced that one "Sues-Anna's". Two special rooms contained a number of mummies of kings and other royal family members of the New Kingdom.

Ed had never even heard of most of the Pharaohs named here. He was, he thought, lost in time and ignorant of it all.

The day came to leave Cairo on the next leg of their journey into the mystery of Egypt. Ed was saying a lot, "It may be his story but is it history?" aware that much of what they were seeing was actually prehistoric.

History was said to have started when a Greek traveller called Herodotus first wrote down some of the stories told for generations around camp fires. Anything before that was called prehistoric and based on word-of-mouth.

<u>1989 LUXOR</u>

So, after a week in Cairo, we flew to Luxor, which in Arabic is called *al-Uqsur*. I was very glad that Ed wore me on his head most of the time, although by now we had such great affinity that I knew what was happening around Ed even when not on his head, I don't think Ed even knew that I was anything but a simple head-covering though. Yet!

We stayed in Luxor in a bungalow in the grounds of a big modern hotel called Sheraton, the same name as their hotel in Cairo. This one was next to the river Nile and very beautiful.

As they stepped off the tourist coach they had taken from Luxor airport, they were greeted by a small group of musicians playing "Happy Birthday to You" on a variety of stringed instruments and a hand drum. They were smiling broadly and all the tourists handed them baksheesh, so Ed did the same.

The five-star hotel was very grand; the foyer was huge and busy with new arrivals and each person was offered a glass of a hibiscus soft drink which Ed enjoyed. They were quickly booked in and were led to their bungalow by a young man who carried their luggage easily. They tipped him.

There was an artificial pool in the hotel grounds and they had to walk past it between the main building where the reception and the restaurants were situated and their bungalow. Six large pelicans lived in and around the pool and often stood on rocks as if posing as Ed and Ana walked passed. "Almost as if they're grinning, definitely showing off", Ed said to Ana.

The evening meals were part of their holiday deal and consisted of serve-yourself buffets with a range of food, washed down with local beer. Ed found the local wine to be undrinkable; it had a smell far worse than the river, certainly not what he called a bouquet.

The first evening, after dinner, Ed read as much as he could about what there was to see in and around Luxor and realised there would not be much time to relax. He made some lists so he could chat to Ana about what they would do the next morning. Ed fell asleep quite late.

Ed was awoken very early in the morning by the sounds from the nearby minaret from which a Muezzin was shouting through a megaphone about how great Allah was and calling the devotees to prayer. Then he heard Ana's voice: "Hello, is that reception? Well there's a lot of noise outside. Somebody is playing a radio or something very loud and it woke me up!"

Ed quickly explained to Ana that the noise was in fact part of the religion and happened more than once every day, to call the people for prayer, and dawn was the first time. We would get it every day. She was like somebody in the UK complaining about church bells. Ana laughed and said "Sorry, I thought it was a radio" to the phone and put it down. I knew now that many places had phones, even from one part of a hotel to another, not like back in 1972 when I had been taken on another head, called Al, whom I mentioned before, to India. In India there were hardly any phones. Human communication had become much more electronic. As a hat, I am not sure if that is all good or all bad or some of each, but that day I imagined that reception wished there were no phones.

I wondered also if there would ever be phones for hats.

Ed never even knew that I was a being and that I had such a good memory. It was all one-way in those days. On the other hand, or head, I had never communicated with another hat and I did not know if those many hats that I had seen even had any story to tell.

I am Myhat, and have many tales.

Now, in Luxor in Egypt on the river Nile, I knew that neither Ed nor Ana knew much about the place, even less than they knew about Cairo.

Ed knew that there was supposed to be a great tomb here, said to have been discovered about a hundred years ago by Howard Carter and to have been the burial place of a boy king called *Tutankhamun*.

He knew it was in a place called The Valley of the Kings on the other side of the Nile, on the West bank where the sun set. He wanted to go there. He also knew, though, that there was supposed to be an ancient curse on anyone who went inside. I wondered if hats would be cursed too.

Ed and Ana sat and made a list of what they wanted to see and do. Looking through the brochures and day trips on offer by taxi or coach, there was a lot to see.

First there were the great temples of Luxor and Karnak.

Those were on the east bank, the same side as the hotel. There was a small local museum.

Across the river there was not only the Valley of the Kings which in fact had many more tombs than just *Tutanhkamun's*. There was also the Valley of the Queens, the Valley of the Nobles, The Mortuary Temples of *Hatshepsut* and *Ramesses*, and his *Ramesseum*, *Medinet Habu*, the Colossi of *Memnon* and the workman's village at *Deir el Medina*. They were all within reach of each other but surely it would take more than one day.

Also, Ana, being fond of boating, persuaded Ed to include an afternoon ride in a *felucca* on the river in their itinerary.

They also chatted about taking a day trip to Aswan to see the dam and some temples on the way.

Also they wanted to see the Souk market and maybe catch some local life.

By the time they finished, there would be little time to laze around the swimming pools as many tourists seemed to enjoy doing.

Of course I never had any say in those plans, not that I would have known what to say, had I the chance. As usual, I focussed on watching, listening and remembering. The name *Hatshepsut* had captured my imagination too.

It was a slow breakfast that first morning and as the day got hotter they decided to take a taxi to Luxor Temple, the smaller of the two big temples in Luxor town itself and then to carry on to the much larger temple complex at Karnak, which was a few miles away, after lunch.

The taxi ride was just a few minutes; they passed many kalesh (local horse and carriages), as well as numerous taxies, buses, cars and trucks. All the traffic movement seemed very random to Ed, just about keeping to the correct sides of the road. They pulled up at an open green area where the entrance to the Temple was situated and they bought their entrance tickets. The taxi driver told them he would wait as long as they wanted and then take them to Karnak.

Luxor Temple was impressive even from the taxi. The columns were clearly very tall and what had survived thousands of years was obviously built well and with great devotion.

As soon as they alighted from their taxi and paid, they were approached by several street hawkers offering papyrus cards, papyrus paper, papyrus bookmarks and small trinkets; many of the hawkers were children that looked no older that ten. They each shouted "Hello mister, welcome to Egypt, you want to buy?" insisting that their goods were genuine. Not that he wanted the stuff, but it was so cheap that he felt he had to buy some. Ana bought some greeting cards made from papyrus and a city map.

They headed towards the entrance to Luxor Temple itself to what was once a very holy place but now just, in fact, a tourist

MYHAT IN EGYPT: THROUGH THE EYES OF A GOD

attraction. The massive stone entrance had a gigantic statue either side and a tall obelisk on one side.

Ed had picked up an information sheet at the hotel and read aloud to Ana, as they sat just inside the entrance.

"Luxor Temple is a large temple complex located on the east bank of the Nile River in the city today known as Luxor or, in ancient times, Thebes and was founded in 1400 BC. It is known in the Egypt also as ipet resyt, or the southern sanctuary.

"Luxor temple is not dedicated to a cult god or a deified version of the king in death. Instead Luxor temple is dedicated to the rejuvenation of kingship; it may have been where many of the kings of Egypt were crowned.

"The temple was built of sandstone. At the Luxor temple, there had been two obelisks. The smaller one closer to the west is now in the Place de la Concorde in Paris. With the layout of the temple they appear to be of equal height, but using illusion, it enhances the relative distances hence making them look the same size to the wall behind it.

Symbolically, it is a visual and spacial effect to emphasize the heights and distance from the wall, enhancing the already existing pathway.

"It has been determined that the Luxor temple holds great significance to the Opet festival. The Luxor Temple was dedicated to the Theban Triad of the cult of the Royal Ka, Amun, Mut and Khonsu. It was built during the New Kingdom as the focus of the annual Opet festival. Inside was a cult statue of Amun which was paraded down the Nile from Karnak Temple.

Ed and Ana wandered about inside, looking at the lofty columns and pylons and admiring the courtyard, taking a few photos along their way. Although it was a massive construction, nothing like the pyramids, it was very impressive. They stayed for just about half an hour. It was already hot and they went outside to get a drink at a small stall they had spotted and then took a look at the Avenue of

Sphinxes. Although many of the stone statues were damaged, Ed thought they were beautiful.

Their taxi was waiting outside and the driver called to them as they reached the road, so they jumped in and headed to Karnak Temple.

There was a short walk from where the taxi dropped us off and, once again, the driver said he would wait. This time he would not take payment and simply said "later".

As they approached the main entrance after buying their tickets, Ed and Ana were again approached by many street hawkers offering papyrus scrolls with beautiful colourful paintings of scenes from stories of the ancient gods and the afterlife; others offered small statuettes of kings and gods, cotton shirts and djellabas, postcards and books whilst one man even offered a ride in a boat across the Nile.

Ed and Ana walked down to what Ed thought was the other end of that Avenue of Sphinxes from Luxor, towards the main entrance which had tall statues on either side of the main doorway portal.

"Ed, I read that the Avenue of Sphinxes is a mile and a half long," Ana said.

"Let's sit here on the wall and I'll read a bit before we go in, 'cos I reckon it's huge and we'll never know what's what."

So Ana read from the information page:

"The Karnak Temple Complex comprises a vast mix of decayed temple, chapels, pylons, and other buildings. Building at the complex began during the reign of Senusret the First in the Middle Kingdom and continued into the Ptolemaic Period, although most of the extant buildings date from the New Kingdom. The area around Karnak was the ancient Egyptian Ipet-isut , The Most Selected of Places and the main place of worship of the eighteenth dynasty Theban Triad with the god Amun as its head."

"I am going to start making a list of all these names and places and stuff, different Kingdoms and dynasties or it's going to get very confusing about who was doing what when!" said Ed.

Ana continued: *"The key difference between Karnak and most of the other temples and sites in Egypt is the length of time over which it was developed and used.*

"The history of the Karnak complex is largely the history of Thebes and its changing role in the culture. Religious centres varied by region and with the establishment of the current capital of the unified culture, a culture that changed several times. The city of Thebes does not appear to have been of great significance before the Eleventh Dynasty and previous temple building here would have been relatively small, with shrines being dedicated to the early deities of Thebes, the Earth goddess Mut and Montu. Early building was destroyed by invaders. The earliest known artefact found in the area of the temple is a small, eight-sided temple from the Eleventh Dynasty, which mentions Amun-Re. Amun, sometimes called Amen. He was identified with the Ram and the Goose. The Egyptian meaning of Amun is hidden or the hidden god.

"Almost every Pharaoh of that dynasty has added something to the temple site."

"It says more about the different temples but I think we should go in now," said Ana.

As soon as they entered through the massive stone pylons, Ed forgot almost everything the pamphlet had explained and was simply in awe of the size of the place, not least the height, width and sheer numbers of stone columns that had presumably once held up some sort of roof.

Of course, I remembered, as I did.

Ed said to Ana: "Just think, Pharaohs and priests walked here. It never used to be open to the public in those days. This was the holiest of places and they had secret ceremonies."

Ed and Ana tried linking arms around one of the columns. They couldn't. The columns were covered with carvings of hieroglyphs.

At one point one of the men working as what Ed had called Guardians of the Temples beckoned Ed over, so he walked over to the man.

"You want to see something very special not for all people?" the Guardian asked. "Small fee and I take you now. But your Queen stay here OK and wait." motioning at Ana.

Ed always was one to explore so, with me still sitting firmly on his head, he followed the man who walked behind a building and started to climb, scramble, up and around until they came out on the very top of what Ed thought to be one of the temples or chapels. It was a bit of a scramble upwards but Ed thought well worth while. From there he had a 360 degree panorama and could see the Sacred Lake and the countryside beyond; he could see the Nile and the West Bank. Ed took some photos, thinking he could maybe put them together as a collage one day. He wanted to sit and absorb the view, but the Guardian was saying they had to go back down. Ed thought it not entirely safe, that climb and descent, and probably illegal. He paid the Guardian who gave a big smile and shook hands and then immediately called over another tourist.

Ana had waited and Ed told her enthusiastically about his expedition. She said she was not keen on heights and glad she had not followed, as she had at first been inclined to do.

They walked on past side-chambers or chapels and statues and spotted the two big obelisks that were standing and then the fallen one; unless of course it had never been raised. Ed didn't know.

Then they reached the Sacred Lake.

The rectangular lake was quite large and the water was blue. Ed could see at the far side were rows of seats in tiers. They walked up the left side and found a place to sit. There was a hoopoe bird standing on a block. It was very tranquil away from all the Guardians and hawkers. They sat in silence for a while, and

Ed read from the information page.

"Karnak Sacred Lake is the largest of its kind and was dug by Tuthmose the Third who reigned from 1473 to 1458 BC. It measures 393 feet by 252 feet and is lined with stone wall and has stairways descending into the water.

"The lake was used by the priests for ritual washing and ritual navigation. It was also home to the sacred geese of Amun: the goose being another symbol of Amun and was a symbol of the primeval waters from which life arose in the ancient idea of creation."

"Wow," said Ed, "everything we read and more and more names I have never heard of before. It's going to be a long project for me to get it all in some sort of order, chronological I guess."

Tired now, the two humans decided to walk back to their taxi and go back to the Sheraton, which is what they did. Ed was pleased to have seen and read about the two big temples.

Karnak was the largest open temple site in the world. He had read that it covered one hundred hectares, larger than many ancient cities, and thousands of years old. In fact, it had been added to and added to for about a thousand years.

"Karnak was not built in a day," he mused.

That evening Ed and Ana enjoyed a meal in one of the hotel restaurants. Ed ordered a bottle of local white wine. Once opened, he smelled the stuff and sent it back. He ordered a bottle of local red and sent that back too. The waiter did not even smell it; Ed thought maybe religion prohibited him from inhaling alcohol, or maybe he simply knew it smelled so bad that it was undrinkable. So Ed ordered local beer instead and, surprised as he was, he found it quite palatable. They had a good meal and an early night, knowing that no doubt the calls to prayer would wake them again at sunrise.

The following morning, Ed and Ana had a slow and prolonged breakfast at the hotel buffet. There was a huge selection of mostly serve-oneself dishes: muesli, porridge and cereal with milk or soya milk or yoghurt, fruits, fish dishes, various breads, cold meats such as lamb and turkey, cooked English-style breakfast including eggs, fried, boiled or scrambled, fried meats, hot tomatoes, onions, courgettes, egg plants, potatoes and the local dish called foul which is mashed cooked beans; there was a whole range of salads and a long line of different cakes as well as pancakes with different dressings. Also a selection of drinks available including local champagne, which they did not try.

Ed ate far too much.

So, after that slow breakfast, Ed and Ana decided to go for a walk along the Nile and head towards the *souk*, an alleyway marketplace.

They left the Sheraton and were immediately approached by a man selling papyrus approached them. They smiled and returned his "hello" and said no. He followed them but they kept saying no. Then a man selling small statues and some children offering postcards supposedly made from papyrus. Other men were inviting us to see their shops, buy spices, change money, go for a tourist trip or even ride a camel or donkey. Every *kalesh*, the horses and carriages, and every motorised taxi that passed tried to get Ed and Ana as customers. I could tell Ed was becoming impatient with what was becoming harassment although he well knew they were mostly trying to make an honest wage or commission.

They walked to a low wall between the pavement and the river and sat down. It was no more than minutes before a young man dressed in a blue tunic approached them. He asked where they were from and how long were we in Egypt and was it our first time and did we like it. He said that his name was Horus and that he was the captain of his own *felucca* boat and pointed to a wooden boat with its tall sails. If they

33

wished, he had said, they could go with him and sail down to the crocodile island and eat a meal that he would cook on board, all very cheap. Three hours.

Ed knew that Ana loved sailing on boats and sure enough she wanted to go. Ed on the other hand, although he had been on boats, had never been sailing, did not swim and had heard about the risk of illness from the water in the Nile. He thought to try to delay what may have been the inevitable few hours sailing by saying that they were heading towards the souk, so maybe some other time. Horus did not seem upset and smiled and said "OK, maybe later. I will wait for you."

Then they chatted about families and Horus recommended they go to the West Bank to see the tombs and temples. Ed and Ana said goodbye and carried on down the road towards the turning to the *souk*. They dodged the street hawkers, boat captains, taxi and *kalesh* drivers, just smiling and saying "no thanks."

They walked as fast as was comfortable towards the *souk*, with Luxor Temple on their left, they spotted what looked like an army of *kalesh* carriages.

"God, look at that!" said Ed, "It's going to be like running the gauntlet and when we get in the market I can see it being a real hassle. You sure you want to go shopping?"

Ana said that she wasn't bothered as there were lots of shops and they had tourist stuff in the hotel shops too. She told Ed that there was not actually anything she really wanted to go there to buy.

So they turned back, and instead went into the large hotel and café across the road from the Nile ,for tea.

It was called the Winter Palace It had been built in the times when Egypt was a colony of Great Britain. It was a large building with a beautiful and clean-looking facade. They walked up steps and around to the grand entrance, inside and through to a grassy courtyard where they saw tables and chairs and then sat down and ordered tea. Ed thought that it was probably six times the price of anywhere else, but cool and pleasant to sit there, just the two of them.

Ana persuaded Ed, then, to walk back to Horus and take a journey in his *felucca.*

Sure enough, Horus was waiting for them, or seemed to be, and waved to them as they approached. It did not take long before they had an agreement on the price, although Ed knew, and he thought Horus knew, he would give *baksheesh* at the end of the trip.

They were soon in the boat, and Ed was surprised to be feeling quite comfortable about that. Horus explained that they would slowly sail up the river to Crocodile Island and they would stop somewhere and he would cook a lunch of fish and salad and rice and not to worry because everything was cooked and washed in bottled water.

Ed thoroughly enjoyed the journey there and back, just watching the riverbanks as they seemed to drift by. It was a calm afternoon. They had only a small problem at one stage when the boat became stuck close to the bank, but Horus' "boy" who was on board quickly jumped into the Nile and pushed the boat away from the bank; Ed thought that the locals must be immune to whatever the bacteria was that posed such a threat to tourists. Ana said she'd had a lovely day too, out away from the salesmen and taxi drivers.

They reached the hotel just as it was getting dark.

The following morning, Ed and Ana decided it was time to see some tombs on the West Bank. The tomb of Tutankhamun was a must, according to Ana, and the best way, they thought, would be by taxi. There were always taxies at the hotel so pretty soon, filled again by a hearty breakfast they set off in a taxi to the ferry. The driver said he would leave his taxi with his brother and they would cross the river by ferry, then get another taxi at the West Bank landing. He said his name was Mustafa, and that he would take them to the Valley of the Kings and then to see a Queen's tomb and some Tombs of Nobles.

It did not take long before they arrived at the car park where the taxi was waiting and soon Ed and Ana were walking up a dusty road towards the tombs in the Valley of the Kings.

They could see ahead of them the pyramid apex to the mountain, which was said to have been the reason that this valley was chosen, in recognition of pyramids being something special in Egypt.

They reached the point in the road where signposted tracks led to the individual tombs. Ed and Ana had already decided to visit the tombs of *Tutankhamun*, *Seti* the First and one of the *Ramesses*.

First they went to *Seti* the First. By now Ed and probably Ana knew that Seti was a powerful warrior Pharaoh, the son of *Ramesses* the First who had founded a new dynasty.

At the entrance of course there was the usual Guardian, this time with a battery powered torch, and as they entered and showed their tickets, he simply followed them talking non-stop, shining his torch where he wished.

"This tomb very big," he said.

"It is one hundred twenty metres along. It was opened by Belsoni, he strong man from Italy, 1817. Everywhere we see beautiful paintings of Seti and the gods."

We walked along corridors and up and down ramps into side-chambers as the Guardian pointed out *Seti* and the gods and goddesses. "Here is *Seti* praying to sun, *Ra*, also *Amun-Re*. There is *Isis*. Here is *Hathor* and there, *Osiris*. Now we see *Hathor* and *Isis* again."

We saw a chamber with pillars where the Guardian pointed out scenes from the 'Book of Gates'. We arrived at the Burial Chamber where the roof had been decorated with stars.

The whole tomb complex was incredible. Ed wondered just how long and difficult it must have been, just to carve this all out, cover so much with detailed depictions and symbols, then probably fill it with treasure and a dead Pharaoh to then be sealed up, as they thought, for all time. He thought about how fortunate it was that the climate here had helped the beauty survive.

There was far too much to comprehend here. Ed vowed to read up on it later.

All too soon they were ushered out, back into what now seemed like incredible bright sunshine. Ed gave the traditional *baksheesh* to the Guardian and they headed back down to look for the sign to the tomb of *Ramesses*.

They spotted a sign that read *'Ramsis* I Number KV16' and followed the path.

This was a much smaller tomb and had apparently never been finished before the king died, according to their new Guardian who led them inside and down quite a long flight of stairs. The walls here were not decorated. The stairs led directly to the actual burial chamber.

Within the burial chamber they saw a red granite sarcophagus. The chamber was not very large at all; there would not have been so much room for treasure. Here the wall paintings were astoundingly colourful and beautiful. There were scenes of the Pharaoh being carried to his burial. They saw images of *Osiris* on one wall, and *Kephri* on the other.

On each side of the entrance, we saw paintings of the goddess *Ma'at* welcoming the deceased king. On the left wall, we saw the king depicted making an offering of two vases of wine to the god *Nefertum* who wears an open Lotus flower on his head. On the right wall we saw more scenes from the 'Book of the Dead' showing the gods in judgement of the dead Pharaoh's soul.

On the back wall there were more beautiful paintings of the gods with the Pharaoh *Ramesses*.

After leaving that tomb, Ed and Ana, once again impressed, headed down towards the entrance to the most famous Pharaoh of all, *Tutankhamun*, one of the few Egyptians kings that Ed had even heard of before this holiday trip.

Well, Ed had read about the supposed curse that was put on all who enter the tomb. Apparently the Earl of Carnarvon had been bitten by a mosquito after leaving the tomb and later died.   He had been a sponsor of Howard Carter who re-discovered the tomb in 1922, Ed knew, and he had not been the only person that entered that had later suddenly died. Of course, Ed considered the hundreds of thousands that had been inside since. But something was niggling him enough, and he was already tired and wanted tea. So he decided to sit on the wall outside whilst Ana went inside.

Ed knew that *Tutankhamun* had been a teenager when he 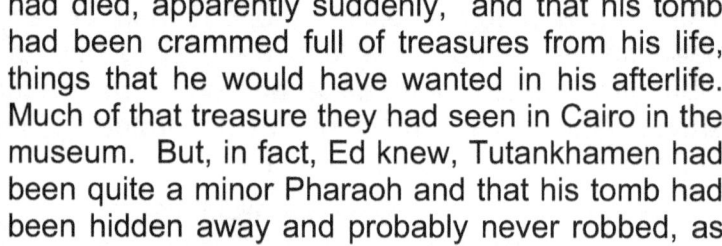 had died, apparently suddenly, and that his tomb had been crammed full of treasures from his life, things that he would have wanted in his afterlife. Much of that treasure they had seen in Cairo in the museum. But, in fact, Ed knew, Tutankhamen had been quite a minor Pharaoh and that his tomb had been hidden away and probably never robbed, as so many others had been.

It was not long after she came back out that Ana had in fact been bitten by a mosquito. They laughed about it, but I felt Ed was a little concerned too. Ana did say that she was really impressed by what she had seen.

I can tell you now though, that Ana did not die from that bite.

Later, they paid a brief visit to the Mortuary Complex of Pharaoh Queen *Hatshepsut* which stood alongside the ruins of the temple of *Mentuhotep* and a few other ruins.

The information pamphlet that they had picked up at the hotel said a bit about that Queen.

"Hatshepsut was a unique female in the eighteenth dynasty who claimed divine birth.

"Hatshepsut came to the throne of Egypt in 1478 BC. Officially, she ruled jointly with Thutmose the Third who had ascended to the throne as a child one year earlier. Hatshepsut was the chief wife of Thutmose the Second, Thutmose the Third's father. She is generally regarded by Egyptologists as

one of the most successful Pharaohs, reigning longer than any other woman of an indigenous Egyptian dynasty.

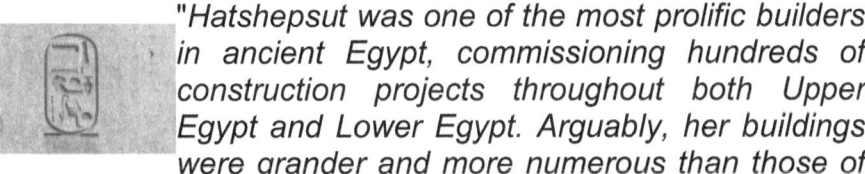 *"Hatshepsut was one of the most prolific builders in ancient Egypt, commissioning hundreds of construction projects throughout both Upper Egypt and Lower Egypt. Arguably, her buildings were grander and more numerous than those of any of her Middle Kingdom predecessors'. Later Pharaohs attempted to claim some of her projects as theirs.*

"Hatshepsut assumed all of the regalia and symbols of the pharaonic office in official representations: the Khat head cloth, topped with the ureaus, the traditional false beard, and shendyt kilt. Many existing statues alternatively show her in typically feminine attire as well as those that depict her in the royal ceremonial attire.

"One of the most famous examples of the legends about Hatshepsut is a myth about her birth. In this myth, Amun goes to Ahmose in the form of Thutmose the First and awakens her with pleasant odours. At this point Amun places the ankh, a symbol of life, to Ahmose's nose, and Hatshepsut is conceived by Ahmose. Khnum, the god who forms the bodies of human children, is then instructed to create a body and ka, or corporal presence or life-force, for Hatshepsut. Heket, the goddess of life and fertility, and Khnum then leads Ahmose along to the bed of the lioness where she gives birth to Hatshepsut. Reliefs depicting each step in these events are at Karnak and in her mortuary temple.

"Hatshepsut claimed that she was her father's intended heir and that he made her the heir apparent of Egypt.

"Claims have been made, and maybe were even at that time, about a possible relationship between Hatshepsut and Senemut, her steward, who was a commoner. His official title translates as "Steward of the Royal Wife". Such a relationship would have been frowned upon and would have been kept quiet. It could have caused a civil war if the Queen's heir was the child of a commoner."

Ed had seen on the map that there was a tomb fairly close by, that had been built for this *Senemut*, so he suggested to Ana that they visit it and she agreed. They had to scramble a little up a hill to get to the tomb entrance which was like a large stone doorway. There was a guardian waiting there and he took them inside with his torch. There were no electric lights in there.

Inside the tomb the chamber had incredible ceiling and wall decorations, full of detail. This was their first tomb of non-royalty. This time Ana read from the hotel's information sheet:

"Senemut was of low commoner birth, born to literate provincial parents, Ramose and Hatnofer.

"Senemut supervised the quarrying, transport, and erection of twin obelisks, at the time the tallest in the world, at the entrance to the Temple of Karnak.

"Senemut claims to be the chief architect of Hatshepsut's works at Deir el-Bahri. Senenmut's masterpiece building project was the Mortuary Temple complex of Hatshepsut at Deir el-Bahari. It was designed and implemented by Senemut on a site on the West Bank of the Nile close to the entrance to the Valley of the Kings.

"The earliest known star map in Egypt is found as a main part of a décor in the Tomb of Senemut. The astronomical ceiling in Senemut's tomb is divided into two sections representing the northern and the southern skies. This indicates another dimension of his career, suggesting that he was an ancient astronomer as well."

That was the last day trip for Ed and Ana. They felt dumbfounded by the amount of information they had tried to absorb. They had met some friendly people and there had been no hostility or problems at all. Most of the locals in Luxor smiled and waved at them, the children, often without shoes and wearing rags, all asked for "*baksheesh*", some few coins or sweets; the older children also asked for "*Ben*". Ana told Ed that they were being asked for pens, as all the children had only pencils and crayons in their poor schools. Sadly though, we did not have *bens* to give them.

This was Ed's first visit to Egypt. I know he was more confused about the almost 2500-year history (mystery) than before he arrived, and he took a year trying to make lists of Pharaohs, Temples, Pyramids and tombs, with dates.

1990: AYMAN

The following year, Ed returned on another tourist package holiday, for another week in Cairo and week in Luxor with Ana. Before they left Norwich,, Ana had given him a gift to open when he arrived. Ed had also purchased a hundred ball-point pens, which he remembered all the locals wanted and called "*ben*".

Ed and Ana were booked on a similar two-week holiday as previously, spending one week in Cairo and one week in Luxor. Ed knew he wanted to see some places again, and some ones additional too.

Ed had started to try to make sense of names and places and dates since his last trip.

When they arrived in Cairo, Ed opened the gift from Ana. It was another hundred "*bens*".

Ed had two hundred pens to give away to the people in Luxor when they were out on the West Bank.

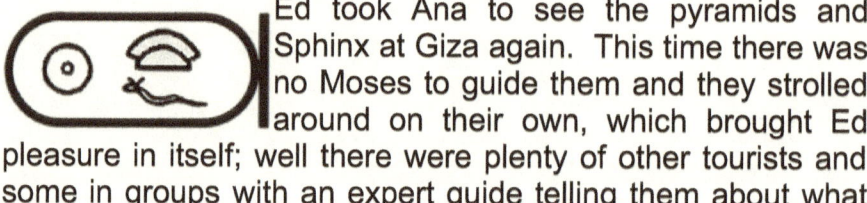 Ed took Ana to see the pyramids and Sphinx at Giza again. This time there was no Moses to guide them and they strolled around on their own, which brought Ed pleasure in itself; well there were plenty of other tourists and some in groups with an expert guide telling them about what they were looking at, and Ed and Ana had a listen too.

The Great Pyramid of *Cheops* also called *Khufu*, was closed to tourists this time, but the second pyramid, supposedly built some five thousand years ago for a Pharaoh called *Khafre* also known as *Kephren*, was open. They also took a look around the outside of the relatively modest-sized Pyramid of *Menkaure* also known as *Mykerinus*, along with a number of smaller satellite edifices known as 'Queen's pyramids'.

A day later, they took a tourist trip to the oasis of Fayoum, also to see the ruins of a pyramid built for a twelfth dynasty Pharaoh called *Amenemhat* the First. Fayoum is about sixty miles from Cairo but it took over two hours, even though the bus was in good conditions and the roads not very crowded. It was a hot ride. The hostess explained a few things about the town.

"*The town occupies part of the ancient site of Crocodilopolis or Arsinoë. It was founded in about 4000 BC, it is the oldest city in Egypt and one of the oldest continuously occupied cities in the world. In the days of the Pharaohs it was called Shedet. They considered crocodiles to be sacred.*

The next day was their last day in Cairo so they decided to spend the morning back at the pyramids, the afternoon in the museum and in the evening they would go by tourist coach back to the Giza plateau for the Sound and Light show.

It was a tiring day and a cold night. The hotel had provided rough woollen blankets and they enjoyed the show. The show was a bit amateurish using what was probably out-of-date equipment. Lights were directed on the pyramids which where quite a distance away from the wooden tiers of seats where we sat. A commentary about the site was broadcast through tinny speakers.

Ed enjoyed it for what it was, as he said to Ana on the way back to the hotel by coach and she agreed.

Soon it was time to take the pre-booked flight to Luxor.

The next day, shortly after leaving the hotel, they were approached by a man who offered donkey-riding days to explore the West Bank. His price was so low that Ed and Ana agreed to meet him the next morning near the ferry crossing and spend a day with him. He said his name was Ayman.

The following day, they set off in the morning to meet their donkey-ride host, Ayman. Sure enough, he was waiting near

43

the entrance to the ferry. He quickly led them passed all the other men offering boat rides, donkey rides or souvenirs, and bought the ferry tickets.

Ed thought it was a bit of a rickety old ferry boat with two levels, that shuddered its way across the Nile. It was quite crowded, mostly what seemed like local people with bundles. Most were dressed in *djellabas* although some young men wore jeans and T-shirts. There were what looked like a few other tourists too.

Upon arrival at the West Bank disembarking point, Ed realised that he was about to enter a quite different Luxor where things appeared to be more basic. The walked up the ramp and followed Ayman a short distance to where two donkeys were being held by a boy. Without many words he helped Ed and Ana to get onto the two donkeys.

Ayman told them "Always wait until I hold donkey before you get on, otherwise maybe problem.

"I take you now on full day trip with lunch. We see Colossi, Temple Hatshepsut, Deir el Bahri, Temple Seti, Medinet Habu, Deir el Medina workmen village and Ramasseum. We have lunch half way. Later we see village life and we see sugar cane and alabaster factory. OK?"

Well, all Ed knew now is that he had heard some of those names but he did not know what was what or where or how old or which Pharaoh had built what or was buried where. I sensed he was keen to learn, so just said "yes", as did Ana.

We set off as Ayman continued talking and chatting about who we were and where were we from and how many children and what do we do in the UK. He called Ana "Your Queen".

First they had to buy tickets at a small kiosk at the side of the road, that would entitle them to enter some of the tombs and most of the temples.

Ed felt surprisingly comfortable on his donkey as they rode past the Colossi of *Memnon*, which Ed read out to Ana were two massive statues that *Amenhotep* the Third had built showing images of himself, which had been just at the entrance to a huge mortuary temple where he would be worshipped after his body was hidden in his tomb in the Valley of the Kings, which they would maybe see one day.

Ed read out some more "*The twin statues depict Amenhotep the Third in about the 1orteenh century BC in a seated position, his hands resting on his knees and his gaze facing towards the river. Two shorter figures are carved into the front throne alongside his legs: these are his queen Tiy and his mother Mutemwiya. The side panels depict the Nile god Hap.*"

"I bet he was happy about that then," laughed Ana.

"*In the twenty-seven century BC, a powerful earthquake reportedly shattered the northern colossus, collapsing it from the waist up and cracking the lower half. Following its rupture, the remaining lower half of this statue was then reputed to "sing" on various occasions – always within an hour or two of sunrise, usually right at dawn.*"

They rode on past the gigantic statues towards the ticket office. Ayman went across and bought the necessary tickets, which were cheap enough.

Ayman explained that our first stop would be at the village of the workmen at Deir el Medina.

The village of the workmen itself was quite large with ruins of houses gathered quite close together.

This time Ana read from her guide book: "*The ancient village was home to the artisans who worked on the tombs in the Valley of the Kings during the eighteenth to twentieth dynasties of the New Kingdom period. The settlement's ancient name was Set Maat which translated as The Place of Truth, and the workmen who lived there were called Servants in the Place of Truth.*

"At its peak, the community contained around sixty-eight houses spread over a total area of five thousand six square metres with a narrow road running the length of the village. The main road through the village may have been covered to shelter the villagers from the intense glare and heat of the sun. The size of the habitations varied, with an average floor space of seventy square metres. Walls were made of mud brick, built on top of stone foundations. Mud was applied to the walls which were then painted white on the external surfaces with some of the inner surfaces whitewashed up to a height of around one metre. A wooden front door might have carried the occupants name. Houses consisted of four to five rooms comprising an entrance, main room, two smaller rooms, kitchen with cellar and staircase leading to the roof. The full glare of the sun was avoided by situating the windows high up on the walls. The main room contained a mud brick platform with steps which may have been used as a shrine or a birthing bed. Nearly all houses contained niches for statues and small altars. The tombs built by the community for their own use include small rock-cut chapels and substructures adorned with small pyramids.

"Due to its location, the village is not thought to have provided a pleasant environment: the walled village takes up the shape of the narrow valley in which its situated, with the barren surrounding hillsides reflecting the desert sun and the hill of Gurnet Murai cutting off the north breeze as well as the view of the verdant river valley.

"The village was abandoned about 1100 BC during the reign of Ramesses the Eleventh, whose tomb was the last of the royal tombs built in The Valley of the Kings, due to increasing threats of Libyan raids and the instability of civil war. The Ptolemies built a temple to Hathor on the site of an ancient shrine dedicated to her."

After leaving Deir el Medina we started ascending the mountain.

Ayman pointed to the right and looking back one could see the Valley of the Queens and further away the mortuary temple of *Ramesses* the Third at *Medinet Habu.*

At the top, Ayman pointed out the connection between the Valley of the Kings and Hatshepsut's Temple much more clearly. It seemed only a short distance between the two. The Valley lay beneath us and we could see what looked like small ants scurrying around going into tombs, the entrances of which we could see clearly. On the other side we could look straight down on the top terrace of *Hatshepsut's* temple and the ramps of the lower levels. We could see the remains of part of the even-more-ancient mortuary temple of *Mentutotep.*

Ed and Ana got down from the donkeys to take in the scenery and take some photographs. The view was simply amazing for them.

Soon it was time to climb back on to the backs of the donkeys. Whilst Ayman was holding the one donkey for Ana, Ed decided he could get on without help, so put his one foot in the stirrup and tried to hoist himself up. The donkey started to move forward. Ed was stuck with one foot in the stirrup with one foot on the ground. He had to hop. He was very close to the edge. I fell off his head and started being blown by the wind even closer to the edge. Ed felt he was about to fall over the edge and I felt I was about to be blown over. By some sort of miracle, Ed thought, or even his guardian angel, there was a wooden post which he grabbed. It was just seconds before Ayman grabbed the donkey's reins and he had somehow even managed to scoop me up on his way. He held the donkey still as Ed managed to get onto its saddle. "I told you," said Ayman, "always wait."

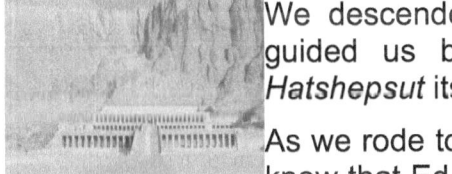 We descended on to a road and Ayman guided us back to see the Temple of *Hatshepsut* itself.

As we rode towards *Hatshepsut's* Temple, I knew that Ed was thinking this must be one of the most beautiful temples that he had ever seen. It had been renovated.

Ed and Ana sat for a while just looking and now it was Ed's turn to read aloud.

"The Mortuary Temple of Hatshepsut was also known as the Holy of Holies and is located beneath the cliffs at Deir el Bahri on the West Bank of the Nile. The temple is dedicated to the sun god Amun-Ra and is located next to the older mortuary temple of Mentuhotep the Second, now in ruins.

"Hatshepsut's chancellor, royal architect Senenmut oversaw the construction.

"Although the adjacent, earlier mortuary temple of Mentuhotep was used as a model, the two structures are nevertheless significantly different in many ways. Hatshepsut's temple employs a lengthy, colonnaded terrace that deviates from the centralised structure of Mentuhotep's model, an anomaly that may be caused by the decentralized location of her burial chamber. There are three layered terraces reaching 97 feet tall. Each story is articulated by a double colonnade of square piers, with the exception of the north-west corner of the central terrace, which employs Proto Doric columns to house the chapel. These terraces are connected by long ramps which were once surrounded by gardens with foreign plants including frankincense and myrrh trees. The layering of Hatshepsut's temple corresponds with the classical Theban form, employing pylons, courts, a hypostyle hall, sun court, chapel and sanctuary.

"The relief sculpture within Hatshepsut's temple recites the tale of the divine birth of a female Pharaoh, the first of its kind. The text and pictorial cycle also tell of an expedition to the Land of Punt, an exotic country on the Red Sea coast. While the statues and ornamentation have since been stolen or destroyed, the temple once was home to two statues of Osiris, a sphinx avenue as well as many sculptures of the Queen in different attitudes standing, sitting, or kneeling. Many of these portraits were destroyed at the order of her stepson Thutmose

the Third, after her death.

"*The main axis of the temple is set to an azimuth of about 116½ degrees and is aligned to the winter solstice sunrise, which in our modern era occurs around the 21st or 22nd of December each year. The sunlight penetrates through to the rear wall of the chapel, before moving to the right to highlight one of the Osiris statutes that stand on either side of the doorway to the second chamber. A further subtlety to this main alignment is created by a light-box, which shows a block of sunlight that slowly moves from the central axis of the temple to first illuminate the god Amun-Ra to then shining on the kneeling figure of Thutmose the Third before finally illuminating the Nile god Hapi. Additionally, because of the heightened angle of the sun, around 41 days on either side of the solstice, sunlight is able to penetrate via a secondary light-box through to the innermost chamber.*"

"Wow what a fascinating place; and a woman Pharaoh," said Ed. "Come on, let's go explore."

So that is what they did, strolling slowly towards and then up the first ramp.

I wondered if this *Hatshepsut* and *Hathor* were anything to do with hats.

Ed and Ana walked towards the temple, passed a short statue of some sort of falcon representing *Horus*, and walked up the stone ramp. At the top there were rows of stone statues, some with heads and some without, some showing residual blue and red coloured areas, all with arms crossed. These were lined up on each side of the entrance. They were at least 15 feet tall.

They were soon approached by a temple Guardian looking for *baksheesh*, no doubt. He quickly said hello and without pause started explaining what was what but in such a way that it was quite meaningless to us. Yet he took control and Ed and Ana followed him. He pointed out that *Hatshepsut* was a woman who claimed divine birth and was often depicted with the head of a cow, like *Hathor*. *Hatshepsut*, he said, had sent an expedition to the Land of *Punt* to bring back precious stones and gold and spices.

The Guardian showed them to what he called the Hathor Chapel and pointed out carvings that showed depictions of Hatshepsut suckling on a cow's udder, dancing for *Hathor* and seated between *Hathor* and *Amun-Ra*.

Nearby he pointed out beautiful *Hathor*-headed columns which were once part of a Hypostyle Hall.

Then he led them to the Temple of *Anubis*, a jackal-headed god. He showed them where carvings that, he said, were of Hatshepsut, had been destroyed.

To one side of the ramps, looking down, they saw a vast array of blocks of stones that looked as if they were waiting to be sorted and put back together. Ed said he thought that must be part of the ruined Mortuary Temple of *Mentuhotep*.

"We'll have to come back here again if we get a chance, there's so much to see but I want to read up about it," said Ana.

After leaving *Hatshepsut's* Temple, they rode their donkeys and stopped at a Temple called the *Ramasseum*, the Mortuary Temple of *Ramesses* the Second. It too was impressive, but by this time Ed for sure was tired and not absorbing much, so they did not stay long.

Ayman said he wanted to take them to an alabaster factory but Ed made it clear that at this time they were tired and hungry and did not want to go. So Ayman told us that we could go to a house in the village for mint tea and then to his house for dinner and to meet his family.

"Let's do that," said Ana. Ed thought he'd be happy if he could just sit on a chair.

The village was called *Al Qunah* and this was the village they had seen from afar. Ayman said that there were tombs under the village and the people were always digging looking to find new tombs and precious things to sell. He said that his brother in the big house would show them some items whilst they had some tea but that there was no need to buy anything. Ed said that he did not want to buy anything.

Inside the house, we met a large chap dressed in a blue *djellaba* and a coloured headscarf. He smiled broadly and motioned Ed and Ana to sit in two armchairs, whilst he sat on a third. Ayman sat on the floor near the door, Minutes later a teenage boy brought in a large brass tray with a brass teapot and brass goblets. Black tea with sugar was poured for all and the boy took a goblet to Ayman; Ed noticed that Ayman took about six lumps of sugar.

Our host said his name was Mustafa. I could tell that Ed immediately felt suspicious of this Mustafa. There was some sort of mischievous or dishonest glint in his eyes. Ed determined himself not to buy anything.

Mustafa showed them a partly-disintegrated wooden figurine representing the dog-headed god of the underworld, *Anubis*. Mustafa said, in broken English, that it was three thousand years old and that it had come from underneath one of the houses here. He told them that people could not buy these in shops and that it was very precious but for them there would be a special price of one hundred UK pounds.

Ed said that he had heard there were a lot of copies and forgeries on sale and that wood could be made to look old by soaking it in tea.

He asked Mustafa: "How do I know it is from the time of the Pharaohs?"

Mustafa said: "My friends, you can trust me. I am an honest man and I offer this to you because you come with my brother Ayman and he says you are good people."

Ed said: "It is so beautiful that I would buy it if it was a replica but If you are saying this is three thousand years old it should be in a museum. It must be more precious than one hundred pounds!"

Mustafa kept the same grin on his face but Ed could see he

was disappointed. He did not even show them anything else, but as they finished their tea he stood up and offered his hand, saying "Bye bye, my friend, you very wise."

After leaving the house and village, Ed and Ana handed out pens, which the locals called bens, to many children but also to adults and, at one point, to a policeman who said "and *ben* for my wife and *ben* for son, mister please."

They set off, again on their donkeys,

At one place along the track and heading for Ayman's family house, they were approached by a young maybe teenage girl who offered them a rag doll; it was simply stitched and stuffed, but colourful enough, probably made from rags but certainly by hand. It had a square head with a funny face. It was very crudely made but then again, thought Ed a rare gift for somebody back home. The first asking price was cheap enough, so he handed over some Egyptian coins and a few *bens* as *backsheesh*.

They rode alongside fields growing crops and suddenly turned off up an even smaller road where there were several houses with small walls around. There were ragged barefooted children playing in the dust and chickens running around pecking at what must have been donkey droppings. Several of the young children ran towards us, greeting Ayman, who proudly said "My children. Come, my friends, my wife will have some food for us ready now. Please come, relax, eat and drink. I will take you to ferry after, before night comes."

Ayman's family house was a small brick building with a small courtyard outside where the donkeys were tethered. Ayman proudly introduced his four boys, who were called Mohammed, Omar, Youssef and Amir; he also had two daughters, Sara and Sofia, the youngest child. The youngest boy, Amir, looked about four years old. There was no sign of Ayman's wife.

First, Ayman brought water to wash, and then plates full of food; chicken, rice, bread, chips, vegetable dips, yoghurt and salads. They all sat cross-legged on the floor and feasted.

The drink was water. Afterwards Ayman supplied fresh figs and sweet cakes with black tea.

Ayman seemed keen to learn as much as possible about Ed and where he and Ana were from; he asked about their jobs and their interest in ancient Egypt.

Ayman offered to take them to the entrance to a secret tomb that had many inscriptions that they could see and copy. He said that the entrance had been used to break into other tombs to look for artefacts, by some of the local people for many years, but now there was little left but the inscriptions. It was possible, he said, for a small fee, to be allowed to go inside.

Their time in Luxor was coming to an end, so Ed said no but promised one day to return to Luxor and see the tomb.

Sure enough, Ed and Ana found themselves back in the cold weather in Norwich, all too soon for them.

Ed thought a lot about what sort of technology and construction methods could have been used to create the magnificent and buildings that we had visited. He could accept that many temples, tombs and obelisks could have been cut using a large labour force, but when he thought back to the time of the Great Pyramid, or at least to the time that they had been built, supposedly, he realised that manpower alone would not solve the problem of time taken.

Ed had read that the Great Pyramid of Cheops or *Khufu* contained an estimated two and a half million stones, most weighing over seven tons, some weighing over twenty tons each. Those stones had to be cut, transported and placed with great accuracy and some had to be raised hundreds of feet into the air.

Egyptologists had written that it was completed in just twenty years and had to be finished when the Pharaoh died. They also claimed that the king had been buried within although there no body was found within.

They had written that a hundred thousand men would have been employed, which of course, Ed reasoned, would have needed a large number of other people such as architects and engineers, foreman and more people to feed them all.

So Ed did a calculation. He worked out how many minutes were in twenty years, assuming that the workmen worked for eighteen hours a day, for every day of the year.

There are 10,512,000 minutes in twenty years.

So, he thought, to place 2,500,000 in 10,512,000 minutes would mean accurately placing a stone about every four and a half minutes.

That, Ed thought, must have been impossible; after all, they were not even supposed to have yet invented wheel or pulley.

That made Ed think that there must have been either some form of stone-age technology that has been lost, or it took a lot longer than twenty years, was not built for the Khufu we talked about, and maybe even built a great length of time earlier than 2,500,BC.

There was, Ed mused, a lot more mystery than history, when it came to ancient Egypt. He was determined to collect what information as he could about those days, try to put it in some sort of order and sense.

BACK TO THE THE NILE

It was two decades before Ed was able to visit Egypt again and, once again, I found myself happily upon his head.

Again he went with his lady-friend called Ana.

He had seen Ana during the last twenty years and they remained good friends through her two unsuccessful marriages.

Ana was fascinated by the tombs and the prehistory.

She was also very clever with languages, including, by now, Arabic and Berber, which she had studied since 1990. She had also studied the ancient Egyptian hieroglyphics and demotic scripts used in ancient times which had been discovered on the Rosetta stone along with Greek. It was the Rosetta stone that first led to a better understanding of hieroglyphs after the time of Napoleon, in 1799.

Ana was slender in build with long red hair which Ed loved; she was naturally friendly, almost flirty, by nature. Ed knew that Ana done a great amount of travelling herself, to India and Nepal, North Africa and many places in Europe, as well as her previous trips to Luxor and Cairo with Ed, Ed thought she was quite capable of looking after herself, but also, feeling that he would do his best to protect her in Egypt.

I felt a little upset that he would put Ana before me, maybe cared more about her. Yet, quite often, he had left me on a chair or table and I had been lucky that somebody reminded him, including Ana; so I also appreciated her myself.

Ed was keen to see how Luxor had changed in twenty years. During those two decades, there had been trouble, even riots, in Cairo and other cities and a terrible incident when a tourist bus was shot at near the Temple of *Hatshepsut* on the West Bank at Luxor and people had been killed. Ed took advice and carefully considered the situation and decided Luxor was still one of the safest places to go. So they booked a three-week stay in a hotel on the West Bank which was closer to the tombs and a more authentic experience; not the standard of the hotels back in 1989 and 1990, but there was everything they needed.

Ed wondered what had happened to Ayman, the man who had taken them on the donkey ride in 1990. Would he still be alive? His children would have grown up by now and maybe even doing their own donkey rides. Ed had brought with him a photo of Ayman and his family taken back in 1990. He asked the guys at the hotel reception if they knew the man but they did not. They agreed, however, to get the photo copied and pass it about; if Ayman was still alive, somebody would know him, or maybe recognise the children.

On their first day, Ed and Ana crossed the Nile and visited the Temples of Luxor and Karnak as well as the Museum of Luxor on the Cornice beside the river. The Museum contained some of the most spectacular and well-preserved statues and artefacts that he had ever seen.

Although Ed had seen both temples several times already, he enjoyed spending the time with Ana again, able to point her to some of the sections and cite some statistics. He showed her the entrance to the climb that he had made at the invitation of a temple guardian, in exchange of course for *backsheesh*, decades earlier when he had been there with Ana. The guardian and Ed had scrambled up to the roof of a huge section from where they had a fantastic panoramic view. Sadly, Ed thought, the entrance was now barricaded.

The Luxor Museum, which cost just a small sum to enter, included entry to a film show and access to the main galleries. Therein, Ed and Ana saw items that had them standing in awe.

Among the items on display were grave goods from the tomb of *Tutankhamun* and a collection of twenty-six statues from the New Kingdom that were found at Luxor Temple. The mummies of the Pharaohs *Ahmose* the First and *Ramesses* the First were also on display. There was a reconstruction of one of the walls of *Akhenaten's* temple at Karnak. Amongst the featured items in the collection was a calcite double statue of the crocodile god *Sobek* and the eighteenth Dynasty pharaoh *Amenhotep* the Third.

That evening they went to Karnak Temple for the Sound and Light show. Again, he had seen the show twice decades before; it had not changed much, Ed thought, but he enjoyed being there again with Ana.

Afterwards they took an excellent but quite pricey fish dinner at a restaurant just down the road, before heading back to cross the river and back to their hotel. It had been a tiring day. They planned to head to *Hatshepsut's* Temple the next morning before it became too hot, then spend the afternoon in the cool courtyard of the hotel.

I wondered again whether *Hatshepsut* was in anyway connected to ancient hats, but I knew Ed and the books believed that her name was connected to the goddess *Hathor*. But why was Hathor so called by that name, nobody knew.

The following morning there was a message at reception to say that the hotel Manager had found Ayman, the donkey owner who had taken him on a ride with Ana twenty years or more earlier. The Manager had left a message to say he could arrange a meeting the next day.

To Ed's surprise and pleasure, the following morning the hotel manager told Ed that he had indeed arranged for Ayman to be brought to the hotel that evening, by taxi as he had problems walking. Also Ayman's son was the taxi driver. Ed thought how strange it would be to meet again.

Ed and Ana went to visit *Hatshepsut's* Temple again. They were surprised to see that the site had been cleaned up to some extent and some restoration work had been done. Ed had always had a fascination with *Hatshepsut*, a female pharaoh that future rulers had tried to erase from history but had failed. Her mortuary temple at Deir el Bahari was one of the most beautiful in all of Egypt. *Hatshepsut* had claimed divine birth and was often represented as the cow-headed goddess *Hathor*. She had dressed as a man, wearing a kilt, false beard and crown. She had had temples constructed and raised obelisks at Karnak Temple on the east bank, sent expeditions south to the mysterious "Land of Punt" and been very powerful in her time. Ed and Ana both had a certain admiration for her although they knew also that she had been a very cruel and powerful tyrant too.

That evening, they took a meal at their hotel and at about seven o'clock, in walked a young man and an elderly man with walking sticks. It was Ayman.

Ed and Ayman first shook hands and then hugged; Ayman introduced the younger man, his son called Youssef, the taxi driver.

Ed felt a great warmth towards Ayman, even though they had met just once twenty years previously; in those days Youssef was just a child. Ed felt that he could trust them both.

Ayman's wife, he said, had died five years earlier; his daughters, Sara and Sofia, were married and had young babies of their own, his other two sons, Mohammed and Omar, were both working as tourist guides. His youngest son, Amir, had sadly disappeared years earlier.

Ayman no longer lived in his little house and now shared a different house in the "new" village belonging to his brother, Mustafa, who was ten years younger.

Ayman, Ed and Ana spent about an hour together, drinking tea and asking and answering questions, and laughing about their lives and how everything had turned out.

Ayman invited Ed and Ana to have dinner at his house the following evening and said that Youssef would collect them from the hotel at six o'clock and bring them back afterwards. Ayman was proud that they had mobile (cell) phones so keeping in touch would be easy. They exchanged numbers.

There were no such phones in Luxor when they had first met.

The following day, sure enough, Youssef took Ed and Ana by taxi to Ayman's house.   Brother Mustafa was not there. Ayman said he that he had gone to Cairo for important business.   He explained that Mustafa had been an English teacher in Cairo, then moved back to Luxor and set up a business in antiques, made a lot of money and bought the house. He did not spend much time there, he said.

Ayman explained that his son, Amir, had disappeared when he was just twelve-years-old;   apparently he and his friend Kareem had last been seen playing near some old houses in the old village. Amir and Kareem had never returned to their homes despite extensive searches including in the tunnels and tombs that lay beneath and connected to the old village houses.   Ayman said that those tunnels had been a secret well-kept by the locals who had used them to find ancient artefacts that they then sold on the illicit market to rich tourists.   Ayman said he remembered taking Ed to the house of such a salesman twenty years earlier It was his brother Mustafa, who had offered Ed a wooden carving of the jackal-headed god Anubis and Ed had said that if it was a replica, he would buy it, but if genuine then it should stay be in a museum in Egypt.   Ayman said that he had thought Ed wise.

Ayman and the authorities believed that his son Amir and Kareem had either been kidnapped, or had gone into the tunnels, fallen into the river or wandered into the desert and gotten lost

Ayman also told Ed and Ana that he could arrange, for a small fee, for them to be shown the entrance to the tunnels and a rough map, but that they should dress in Djellabah's, take some torches and spare batteries;   also, he said, they should take some chalk to mark their way and notebooks and pencils if they wanted to copy the inscriptions, which there were plenty of, but he did not think they would find much in the way of artefacts from the time of the Pharaohs.

"Maybe some old Pepsi Cola cans or cigarette packets!" laughed Ayman.

Dinner was served and they sat on the floor eating with their hands: a local feast of chicken, salads, dips, bread, French fries and rice, yoghurt and fresh figs.

Afterwards, Ayman told his "boy" to bring tea with milk (most tea in drunk Egypt was not with milk), with biscuits and sweet stuff that Ed had never seen before.

Ayman asked if Ed and Ana smoked Alfalfa.

Ed never knew that plant could be smoked and wondered what it would be like. However, when Ayman passed Ed a metal tin with a green plant material inside it, Ed soon realised that it was, in fact, cannabis buds.

So Ed and Ana spent the next couple of hours smoking the cannabis plant along with Ayman and Youssef. Ed did not think that the cannabis was very strong, probably a good thing as Ayman explained that almost everyone there grew and used the plant, sometimes to ease pains but also just to relax.

They chatted about how Luxor had changed since Ed had been there twenty years previously with Ana. Ana. Ana was able to speak with them in Arabic and help with translation and explained how the whole world had changed. Luxor had many new buildings and many more people, like so many other places and, being a major tourist attraction, the emphasis now, said Ayman, seemed to be on the big hotels who charged more for one night than the average worker earned in a month. Of course, business had boomed for kalesh and taxi drivers and also the *felucca* men. But, he said, the number of kalesh and taxies had already grown so, at many times, especially in the summer when there were less tourists because of the heat, there were many drivers just sitting in hope for a fare. In the summer, many hotel rooms were empty and they had to lay off staff, so there were many unemployed and poor people in the summertime.

After a brief chat, Ed and Ana decided to take up Ayman's offer and explore the tunnels. It was to be in two days time and they would be taken to the house where the entrance to the tunnel was hidden in the garden at the back, setting off just before dawn so they would not be spotted by police or official tourist authorities. They said their good nights. "Mighty Night" said Ayman.

Sure enough, two days later, as planned, at five o'clock in the morning, Youssef arrived at the hotel. Ed and Ana had donned *djellabas* on top of T-shirts and jeans. Ed took a small bag with his ID, some money, a torch, a box of matches and some pieces of chalk; also a ball of string which he could use to mark their way in the tunnels if they were damp; a bottle of water and some biscuits to eat. He took his mobile phone too. I was very glad that Ed decided to wear me that day too; I never would have guessed just how glad I was to be.

Youssef explained that he would show them the concealed entrance to the tunnels but that, as far as he knew, nobody had been inside for a long time; they should not expect to find any "old pieces" but they would see inscriptions inside the tombs. There were several tunnels leading to several tombs. Of course, he said, they must be careful not to get hurt or cause anything to collapse, although the tunnels had been there for decades without incident since they were built.

When they came back outside the tunnels, they should cover the entrance again and they should try not to let anyone see them leave the house, but once outside the house it was OK, he told them.

"And," he said, "If policeman sees you then say you are tourists exploring but do not say about me or father, then do not worry, you will be OK."

The journey to start of the bottom of the hill which led to the house was only minutes; they could have walked.

They scrambled up the hill. The house was boarded up and looked quite ruined, as did the other houses. It was just starting to get light.

Following Youssef around the side of the house to the back, they entered what was probably once a garden. They had to squeeze through a rough wooden fence. They helped him move some old garden pots that were broken, and some rusty corrugated iron that was probably once part of an out-building that had collapsed. Behind that, he showed them a wooden door which was laying on the ground, and when they moved that, they saw the entrance.

The tunnel went down almost vertically for what looked like twenty feet, as Ed could see in his torchlight.

Youssef showed them a rope ladder and how to attach it to pegs in the ground by the tunnel entrance. He told them again to be careful. He said that when they got back out, they should put the rope ladder back and cover the entrance with the door. Then they should phone him and go back to the hotel. He would hide the entrance again later.

Ed climbed through the hole in the ground and started to climb down the ladder. It was only a few steps before he knocked me off his head and I went falling down into the darkness. Oh how I wished he'd get some sort of strap to keep me on his head at times like this.

Before I knew it, I was alone at the bottom of this horrible place. Ed and Ana may well have been in places like this before, on rope ladders, but I had never enjoyed it when I was there. I remembered the time Al, my previous head, had climbed up the side of a ship that was bobbing up and down in the Mediterranean, the day he had left Antalya in Turkey, on his way, at that time, to Beirut. That was back in 1972. I was on his head, the wind threatening to blow me off into the sea, as Al had climbed from a small fishing boat and ascended the ladder. Al could not swim and, as far as I know, neither can I. Yet he obviously made it to the top.

I also remembered Ed descending a ladder near the Great Pyramid twenty years earlier, down into the darkness, not so many steps, and turning back upwards, never to reach the bottom where the tomb was supposed to be. But at that time he had no good source of light, now he had a torch.

I had hope.

My hope paid off, for it wasn't long before I sensed Ed was still climbing down the ladder and … standing on me! I was not happy about that, I can tell you. He should learn to be more careful!

As he picked me up, dusted me off and put me back on his head, I realised, once again, that Ed was more concerned about Ana than Myhat.

Now, with Ana besides him, they headed down the underground corridor.

The tunnels were not high enough to walk upright. They did not have the feel of real ancient tunnels, being roughly hewn with wooden roof supports and a lot of rubble with trash on the ground. They were not level either.

Of course they were completely dark without the torches.

Ed drew arrows on the wall, pointing back the way we had come, as we passed more rough-hewn stone corridors on either side. Ed thought they may have led to tomb chambers, but he and Ana agreed to see how far the main corridor would go, first, seeing the side chambers on the way back.

At one point they almost missed a tunnel which went off from a small chamber that they arrived in. There were inscriptions on the walls, some looking very ancient and some with names and modern dates. It was as they looked back behind them that they saw two tunnels going, seemingly, in the same direction. Ed was keen to mark the correct passageway to take on their return. He wondered where the other tunnel would lead but decided to "check that out later" as he said to Ana.

They continued along the main corridor until they reached another chamber which was blocked off on all sides; the way they had come was the only way in and out of this chamber. It was blocked by what looked like a large bolder, put there almost deliberately, thought Ed, and on the bolder was an inscription.

As the duo shone their torches on the inscription, Ana said that she would try to read what it said.

"Something about danger of death from what has gone before... that the great must rise towards the skies but only the Just will prevail. This is Anubis, the jackal-headed god of the dead," she said.

"Look there is Ra, shining upon the king."

"There's not much else here," said Ed; "let's head back and check out the side-rooms and corridors. We haven't been here even an hour yet," I guess.

"OK," said Ana, "but first can we just turn off the torches and sit for a while, see what it feels like. I think that inscription could be thousands of years old, judging by the style."

So they turned off their torches and sat quietly in the dark for some minutes.

"It's not completely dark," said Ed suddenly, "I can still see your outline. Look there! There's some light seems to be coming from behind that boulder: maybe there's another tunnel! We may have somehow linked up with one of the tombs that is open to the public and has electric lighting in its corridors."

"Well, we've been in here for almost an hour, I reckon but I don't think we've moved far enough to be anywhere near the Valley of the Kings yet. I can't get a signal on my phone, even the clock isn't working, but we're under a big hill so I am not surprised. I wonder if we can climb up and look through?" said Ana

Ed climbed up the side of the boulder and was able to squeeze through a gap; sure enough there was daylight. In fact, it looked like the daylight was coming through a gap along the top of another large boulder. He called through to Ana who, very nimbly, thought Ed, quickly joined him.

They climbed up to the top of the next boulder and could see through and, sure enough, could see the world outside the tunnels. There were green fields of crops, tended by a few workers, and beyond they could see the Nile.

As they walked outside. Ed looked back, and used his chalk to mark the boulder, which, looking back, he realised was quite difficult to distinguish from the other boulders along this side of the hill. The exit through which they had climbed was invisible from just yards away.

"Don't want to get lost," said Ed, "although I guess we'll just have to walk round the hill to get back to the village."

"It looks very different from here," exclaimed Ana.

"Look, there's the fields going up to the river, but on the other side there's what looks like a town but it's not Luxor. But there's no sign of the Luxor Temple and further up the river I would have thought we could see Karnak from here. There's just one or two buildings there. And not a lot of boats and no *fallucas* at all? No buildings at all, no tourist boats or hotels on the other bank. Where the heck or we?"

"I'll ring Ayman and ask him what's going on, where we are. We can't be far away but this view just doesn't make sense." So Ana took out her mobile phone.

"The phone's not working, it won't even switch on," she said. "We'll have to walk down the hill to the field, maybe we'll get a better signal or something, down there. We should do, it worked in the village and on the East bank too. Let's go and chat to that guy in the field."

As they walked, Ed took out his own phone.

That was not working either.

OO – ARE – SET

Ana pointed to a worker who was doing something amidst a field of green crop. He was wearing just a loin cloth. It was very hot, much hotter than Ed had expected for quite early in the day. Ed felt overdressed in the *djellaba* over his jeans and tee-shirt, with me still clinging onto his head.

When they reached the worker, Ana spoke to him in Arabic.

The man shrugged and said something back. He was staring straight at me; I knew that I fascinated him and he wanted me on his head – not that Ed knew, but I would not have minded for a while, just to see through the man's eyes.

"He's saying hello, I think," Ana said, turning to Ed.

"It's not Arabic though, it's more like Berber, the language they still speak in the desert in Morocco. I didn't know they spoke it here. I'll try and ask him where we are."

Ana tried a few words and pointed around the place where they stood."

The man pointed across the river and said "Oo – are – set."

Ana looked at him and pointed also across the river. She said "Luxor?"

The man shrugged and said "Happy".

Ana said said something that was not English and smiled. "Temple of *Hatshepsut*?" she asked.

Another shrug.

"Temple Karnak? *Ramasseum*?"

No response to that, just a big smile on his face and a small bow.

"Oo – are - set! Oo – are - set!" he said pointing and laughing.

"I don't know those words," said Ana, "maybe it's somebody's name, like his boss? Or just an oo - are"

"Oh well," said Ed, "From what I can guess, if we go round the hill we should find the road back to the village or at least see something familiar. It's kind of weird here. It doesn't look at all right. I just can't fathom where we are."

They bowed slightly to the smiling man and set out to walk around the end of the hill that covered the tombs and tunnels they had passed through. From there, Ed thought, they should be able to see Luxor and the Temple.

In fact they did see a town spread out on the other side of the Nile, quite a large place but it was certainly not Luxor.

There were no big buildings or hotels, no Temple, just what looked like a palace. There were no tourist cruise boats moored there, no *feluccas*, just small craft, going back and forth across the river. There was no ferry.

Ed was quite stressed out by now, I could tell, and I too was getting concerned that they were lost. Yet this side was not exactly a huge area, just fields between the hills and the river.

It just looked like somewhere completely different, as if they had exited the tunnels many miles up or down stream, somewhere they had never been before. They found no road, saw no trace of human habitation except for the few men working in the fields.

"The phone's still not working," said Ana, "I think we better go back and find that boulder and get back to Ayman and find out what's going on. Maybe he knows where we are. Maybe he has been here himself."

They walked back round the hill and scrambled up to find the chalk marks.

As Ed was about to climb through the gap above the boulder with the chalk mark, Ana asked "Is this yours?"

She passed Ed a small lighter which had a picture of the pyramids on. Ed flicked it, but it didn't work. He put it in his pocket anyway.   It was a very hot day and I knew that Ed was keen to get back into the cool tunnels.

They quickly climbed back into the tunnel and followed the chalk marks, much faster than it had taken them coming this way, not stopping so much. There were several other tunnels leading off at points, so I sensed Ed was glad he'd marked the way. He had not noticed them all on the way through.

Just about half an hour later, they exited through to the garden in the dilapidated house.

"I'll phone Ayman," said Ed.

As he looked at his own mobile phone, he said "Well I get a signal but my phone says it's only eight-thirty"

Ana checked her own phone. "Weird, mine too. But it must have been two o'clock at least when we turned back, the sun was really high and I'm sure we were away for longer than that. We've definitely been gone for more than a few hours. It took over an hour to get through to the other end and we were there for at least four hours."

Ed phoned Ayman and said that they were back but that they had a problem so would like to meet him again later.

Ed and Ana left the garden, covering once again the entrance to the tunnels behind them.

They walked back to the hotel; sure enough it was only late morning.

They had black tea with milk and a late breakfast of corn flakes with milk, eggs and bread and sweet cakes and orange juice. They were both very hungry.

Ed took out some maps of the area and began scrutinising them.

"I can't work this out at all," he said, "whichever way we went and wherever we came out on the hillside, we ought to have been able to see Luxor and the Temples and we should have found the road. And I don't know why there weren't any boats. There aren't any towns that size for miles"

He decided to walk the short distance from the hotel towards the river. Ana said that she wanted to take a rest so he went alone.

Ed saw everything was as as it should be. There was the river, the ferry and, on the East Bank, he could see the cruise boats and Luxor town along with its Temple and tall lush hotels. Plenty of people about too, as usual, carrying on their daily business, taxies and trucks, donkeys pulling carts.

Puzzled still, he went back to the hotel.

Ana said that Ayman had phoned her to say that Youssef would pick them up at six o'clock.

"I've been thinking about what that guy said. You know when he pointed and said Oo – are - set?

"Well there's nowhere here called that and I asked the manager at reception if he knew anyone called that or any place and he said no. But he said that centuries ago the old place was called *Waset* even before it was called *Thebes.*"

"I looked it up and he's right but that was four thousand years ago, in the time of Pharaohs *Senusret* the First and *Amenemhat* the Second."

Ah, another Hat, I thought, maybe an ancestor. Remember dear reader, that I had also heard of a woman Pharaoh called *Hatshepsut*, who also had a temple built here.

Ana continued: "The books say they were Twelfth dynasty, after *Mentuhotep* the Second, Eleventh dynasty. They'd had a war with the North which lasted for about fifty years and then many of the *Nomes* were united. The town was called *Waset. Waset* was a Goddess."

"Maybe what we saw was some sort of touristy replica or

something, but it must be a huge site. We"ll ask Ayman about it this evening," said Ed.

"Pretty weird. I'm going to ask Ayman if we can go back; we'll cross the river and find out what's going on," said Ed.

That evening, Youssef arrived at the hotel a little after six o'clock and took the pair to Ayman's housed again. His brother, Mustafa, was still in Cairo on business, but would return maybe in a few days time, but, he said, Ed and Ana should indeed go back to the tombs and explore beyond, for he himself knew of nowhere or nobody with the name Oo - are – set or *Waset*. Youssef did not know the name either.

Once again, Ayman's boy brought in a small feast, this time fried fish with vegetables, chips, rice and bread, with a selection of fruit and, this time, Ayman proudly announced that he had "Ingleese teas with milk from cow".

Once again, after eating, they sat smoking the green buds and leaves from locally-grown cannabis, chatting away about what they had seen and about how Luxor had changed in twenty years.

Ayman said that Youssef would meet them and take them back to the entrance to the tunnels early in the morning in two days time.

That would give Ed a chance to check out all the old maps of the area to try to work out where they had been.

Ayman explained that there was certainly no tourist exhibition in the area. He said they should look again for the roads and agreed that they should take the ferry across the river, or another boat, and find out the name of the town.

He said that he was thinking and wondering if that was where his son Amir had gone to years ago and even had a "little hoping" that they would bring him back, even though now he would be a man of about twenty years of age.

Ed showed Ayman the lighter that Ana had spotted outside

the exit boulder.

"It has a picture of the pyramids on it but no gas. I'll give it to you. I guess it doesn't mean much but it was the only thing we found.

"Funny thing to find right there, though, right outside the exit boulder. So it's a small memento but in the distant future it may mean more for your descendants, it will be antique!" Ed laughed.

"Mighty Night", said Ayman.

The following day they crossed the Nile by local ferry, always filled with locals and people touting tourists for trade for taxi or *felucca* trips.

They planned to go to the small house of a man whom Ayman had called "Professor Bertie" and who, Ayman had said, had several old maps of the area around Luxor and other places along the Nile.

"If there is place now called *Waset* or Wasat or anything like that, he would know.

"In Arabic, Luxor we call *al-Uqsur*. It sounds similar but not like *Waset*."

Ayman said the man's name was Albert but he was called by most people as Professor Bertie and he was "Ingleese".

SALEEM AND CINDERELLA

Ayman had told Ed and Ana that they would be met by a *kalesh* driver called Saleem who would recognise them and meet them at the ferry port on the East Bank. He would take them around the town and to the house of Professor Bertie, wait for them and then bring them back to the local ferry.

As they were getting off the ferry and starting to climb the steps leading up to the Cornice, the road that ran beside the Nile at that part of town, they spotted a man wearing a brown d*jellaba* who was smiling and waving at them.

He quickly descended the steps to greet them with a broad smile and handshake, saying that his name was Saleem. He led them back up the steps and kept away the other men touting for trade, almost as if we had become his property. He said he would show them around "real life Luxor, where people live" as well as the *souk*, the marketplace and take them to the Government shops. After that he would take them for lunch in a "cheap local-not-tourist restaurant" and, after lunch, take them to the house of Professor Bertie.

Ed said that they had been to the Government shops before and did not want to go but that they would go to the *souk,* then go to Luxor Museum, have lunch and then see Bertie.

They climbed aboard the *kalesh*, with Saleem sitting in front driving the horse. Ana commented that the horse looked healthy and well-fed. Saleem said: "She called Cinderella, my best horse; very good girl. I have another horse and she named Black Isis."

Before they even knew it, within minutes they had arrived at the *souk*. Saleem said that they should walk through the first street where shops were selling souvenirs, then at half-way point he would meet them with the *kalesh and* drive through the "local market".

So that is what they did. As they climbed down from the *kalesh*, Saleem said to Ed "I like your hat. You give to me as gift?"

Ed just said "No chance!" and pulled me down firmer on his head. I gripped tighter. I did not want to go with a *kalesh* driver. I wanted to go to Oo – are - set.

They walked fairly quickly through the *souk*, not wanting to buy much. Yet as they walked past one of the shops in a row of shops selling tourist souvenirs, Ed spotted and then bought, with very little bartering or haggling as was the custom here, a small statuette of the Pharaoh *Akhenaton*, black, made out of basalt; I know he had wanted one for twenty years at least. I wanted him to buy a statue of *Hatshepsut*, but he didn't. Ana bought some silk pyjamas and Ed looked forward to seeing her wearing them.   She told him: "I'll wear them under the djellaba when we go back tomorrow, they'll be much cooler."

They had seen pyjamas on one of the many stalls but none of the correct size, so the young man working on the stall offered to take them down the street to a shop where they had more variety. So they followed and inside the shop were offered a whole range of silk and cotton pyjamas.   Ana did well to haggle down the price from two hundred and fifty Egyptian pounds for one set to one hundred for two sets. Ed was very pleased to see that.

Then the man who had taken us to the shop asked for *baksheesh*. Ed gave him ten Egyptian pounds.

Then he asked for *baksheesh* for the young man working in the shop, as he said did not earn much money and it was not his shop. So Ed handed over another Egyptian ten pound note. Ana laughed and said "Purchase tax!"

They walked along to the half-way point, not stopping to buy anything else. Saleem was waiting in his *kalesh*. They boarded and he drove them along the rest of the market which was less touristy. They drove past people offering spice, and stopped outside an open-fronted shop where Ana bought several packets of spice, including green peppercorns, saffron and some unknown spice that the salesman called "Egyptian Viagra".

Further up the street they drove past shops selling clothing, tools and foodstuff. Saleem gave a running commentary: "Chickens, meat, flowers, silk and cotton cloths, fishes, rice, beans, bread ...", most of which we on open display on stalls, in dishes or hanging. It was quite a smelly place and quite crowded and several times people had to move things out of the way so we could get along in this narrow track in our *kalesh*.

Then Saleem drove us back along a main road towards Luxor train station, turning off to drive us through narrow streets of old and simple-looking houses of several stories, streets filled with rubbish and smiling, waving, ragged children. Ed had read somewhere that parents had told the children not to beg or ask *baksheesh* as they had years earlier. So instead they shouted "hello" or "welcome".

It was quite smelly and very dusty.

Finally the *kalesh* pulled up outside a restaurant close to Luxor Temple. Saleem asked what they wanted to eat and Ed said fish or chicken. Saleem said that they should allow him to pay the bill and later they could pay him, as it would be cheaper.

Inside the restaurant, they went upstairs. Saleem ordered the food: it was to be chicken. The food arrived and Ed was not surprised to find the chicken accompanied by French fries, rice with little bits of fried onion, breads, hummus and other dips and a tomato and bean salad.

As soon as Saleem had eaten his fill, which was not much, he said he would pay the bill and wait outside and feed Cinderella.

As Ed and Ana were about to leave, some ten minutes or so later, the waiter came to them and said "Bill Sir is one hundred twenty pounds for all."

"Oh I thought the *kalesh* driver had paid." said Ed.

"Yes yes, he paid. I only want you to know how much!"

Ed thought the price reasonable although they left more food than they had eaten, yet he knew that it was probably cheaper for locals, just as is almost everything else in Luxor.

When they were outside, Ed asked Saleem how much but Saleem just said "No problem my friend, you pay me later."

He was feeding the horse on what looked like grass.

PROFESSOR BERTIE

Saleem took them through the back streets towards the outskirts of Luxor, and pulled up outside a new-looking two-storey building surrounded by a green and well-attended garden. "Professor here", he said.

Ed and Ana climbed down from the carriage and Saleem said he would wait. They walked through two large open decorative iron gates, along a short path between the lawns and flower beds, up a few stone steps and were about to knock on the door when it opened.

A middle-aged man with almost no hair and long black beard stood before them with out-stretched hand, which they shook as he said "Hi, I'm Bertie. From London. Welcome to Egypt and my house."

Bertie explained that he had moved to Luxor five years previously, bought this house which had been quite run-down and employed local workers to turn it into what it was today. He showed them around; on the ground floor there was a large reception room with table and chairs, a settee and cushions on the floor; it was dimly lit but had brightly-coloured throws hanging from the wall; it felt quite cool compared to outside. Bertie led them through another door into a large kitchen complete with what looked like a well-stocked bar. The Kitchen opened, at the other end on to a smaller room and off that, to one side, was the bathroom and on the other side a door led to a terrace with easy chairs and a hammock. He took them back inside through the kitchen and opened another door; beyond that, to Ed's surprise, was a home cinema with a dozen of so comfortable chairs.

He led them back to the main reception room, opened another door and led them up some wooden stairs. Up there was another bathroom, toilet and three bedrooms, each with a door opening onto a balcony. The main bedroom had another set of stairs leading to the terrace on the roof, filled with small bushes and flowering plants, along with adjustable sun beds and chairs.

The view was amazing. They could see a large part of Luxor, with Luxor Temple on one side and Karnak Temple on the other. They could see the hills on the West Bank, just able to make out what was probably the Valley of the Kings and the *Mentuhotep* and *Hatshepsut* mortuary temples.

"Wow this place is just incredible!", exclaimed Ana.

Bertie led them back downstairs and out to the back terrace. He turned to a young teenager boy and told him in English to bring black tea with milk, cakes and hasheesh.

The three of them sat down in the shade of the trees as Ed explained that they had come to Luxor for the third time, from Norwich where they lived, in England. Bertie said he knew Norwich well but had himself lived in London, where he had been running a secret club for rich pop stars and actors: he dropped many names of people who had been in his club.

He had moved to Luxor because, he said, he was fed up with London and he was happier here. The locals called him a Professor but in fact he wasn't; just an educated and travelled man.

Ed and Ana excitedly explained to him their experience beyond the tunnels. They did their best to explain the appearance of the town which should have been Luxor itself, telling of the worker who had pointed and said Oo – are – set.

The tea arrived, Bertie filled a small pipe with some light-coloured hasheesh which he said had come from Sudan and, as they sat and smoked and sipped, explained that there was in fact nowhere close to Luxor of the size and appearance they had described.

"I know a lot of people here," he said, "but nobody called that. They call the city here *al-Uqsur*, which is the name in Arabic. Before that it was called *Thebes*. But before that it was called *Waset*"

Ed interrupted: "the only thing we came up with was *Waset*, which is what it was called here, but that was thousands of years ago. That doesn't make sense. It's not like we're time-travellers", he laughed.

They did not reach any conclusions, despite the hasheesh which inspired a lot of imagination and speculation, including the idea that the exit boulder was some sort of TARDIS, a time and space travelling ship used by the fictitious Doctor Who, a highly-successful TV series spanning decades. They laughed a lot about that and the prospects of going back and forth in time. Ed told Bertie about the lighter with the pictures of the pyramids on, that they had found outside the exit boulder and that he had since given to Ayman.

"That's it then," laughed Bertie, "Doctor Who is a smoker!"

A couple of hours later they left, with no solution to the mystery and with Bertie saying he would like to join them on a future trip, but not the following days as he was going to be quite busy.

Saleem was still outside waiting in his *kalesh* and quickly took them back to the boarding place for the ferry.

Once there, Ed asked Saleem how much the restaurant bill was.

He said "Two hundred pounds for the day and two hundred and forty pounds for the lunch."

Ed immediately knew that Saleem had doubled the price of the food, but handed over 500 Egyptian pounds saying "Plus little *baksheesh* for Cinderella."

Saleem smiled broadly and gave them a scrap of white card with his name and phone number written on it and said "My Fader, I am always here when you need to make another journey, only phone to me and I will come. You want go further, I will get taxi. Or you want to fly to Cairo for pyramid visit or Abu Simbel, I will do that all for you too."

Ed liked Saleem and could see that he looked after his horse well, so did not begrudge the money.

"One day you come my house meet my family and we will give you food, my wife will make fry chickens."

Ed and Ana, led by Saleem who cleared their way of young men touting for trade for taxies and boats. They were soon aboard the ferry, across the river and back in their hotel room.

The remainder of the day was spent resting, chatting, eating and sleeping.

That evening Ed and Ana went to the rooftop gardens of the hotel, where several lounge chairs and low tables were laid out.

Instead they lay on the woollen mats and cushions on the ground. It was a full moon that night. I was on top of Ed's head, as usual, as they lay and smoked many pipes of the *hasheesh* that Bertie had given them.

They also drank a few bottles of the local beer.

Ed felt warm and cosy, glad to be there with Ana. He wanted to get closer and closer to her as they chatted about the possible interpretations of their experience beyond the tunnels and their talks with Ayman and Bertie.

They shared ideas on what would happen if they went back and asked each other how long should they stay and what should they take with them. Ana said she had wondered about the significance of the lighter she had found. She told Ed that she wondered who would have left that lighter there and thought it important.

All too soon it was the next morning and they found themselves walking with Youssef towards the house on the hill and then climbing down the ladder back into the tunnels.

Ana wore her new pyjamas, as she has said, under her *djellaba*.

Ed had decided to wear just his underpants beneath his. He carried a small leather bag containing his phone, torch, candles, matches and chalk, a small notebook and pencils and a bottle of mineral water.

He also had several hundred pounds in Egyptian money and some coins which was customary to hand out to tomb guardians and guides. I was on his head and he managed to climb down the rope ladder without knocking me off again as I clung on tighter than ever.

They walked through the tunnels faster this time, following the previous chalk marks and were soon, once again, standing beyond the exit boulder. It was still dark.

It seemed darker than when they had climbed down the ladder but it was now starting to get light here too. Ed thought that was just another mystery as they sat looking across the river to the town that appeared again as the morning mist was dissipated by the already warm sunshine.

Since it was light enough, they headed down the hillside and towards the river to look for a way to get across it.

It took almost an hour for them to reach the river; they walked slowly. It was getting hot fast and Ed was glad, I knew, to have me on his head shading his eyes, even though his spectacles, as usual, darkened in the bright light. Now, Ed realised, they were back in the different world, far from Luxor. Maybe, he mused, even a different age.

They arrived at the river bank where some small wooden boats were moored. As they approached, the man who sat in one waved to them to climb aboard. As soon as they were seated he started to row across the river using two long wooden oars. It did not take more than a few minutes.

As Ed looked back across the river towards the West Bank, he could see the place where he knew *Hatshepsut's* temple should be but instead of that, set in the cliffs was another temple. He wondered if it was representing the Temple of Mentuhotep.

Funny, he thought, when we were in Egypt in 1990 I really wondered what *Mentuhotep's* temple would have looked like before it had been destroyed and the newer temple of *Hatshepsut* was built alongside and partly in front of it, using some of the materials.

As Ed stood up ready to climb ashore, he handed the man a small Egyptian bank note, ten pounds. The man looked at it and smiled. He held it up to the light. He folded and unfolded it. He bowed and placed in beneath his short garment. He pointed ashore and said "Abam – ee – ra."

Ed asked Ana if she knew what that meant. She responded that she did not know for sure, but often in Arabic they put 'Ab" before somebody's name to indicate that it was somebody's father; so, she said, in this case it could mean the father of Am - ee – ra. Like the name Amir, but with the 'ra' added.

Ed mentioned that it was coincidence that Ayman's missing son had been called Amir and now the first person they were being sent to, if in fact it meant a person's name, was quite similar.

"So," said Ed, "my father would be Abed?"

"Guess so," she laughed.

Ed laughed. "And Ana means sexy one!"

"Maybe," she said, "but it also meant 'goddess'."

"Sexy goddess, then," he said.

ABAMIRA

They climbed some stone steps to the top of the bank where they saw some sort of ceremonial-dressed guard wearing a purple tunic over a brown kilt, a dagger at each side and carrying a spear. He bowed to them. He seemed to have been expecting them.

Ed said "Abam-ee-ra" and the guard motioned for them to follow him.

They were led towards the centre of the town which seemed to be consist mostly of mud huts, in the direction, as Ed thought, of the palatial-looking building they had seen from the other bank of this river.

They were joined by six other men, dressed in brown kilts, carrying spears, clubs and knives. They each wore a purple sash across their chests. They said nothing.

There were many people around, some leading donkeys, others carrying things. Most of them were men, dressed in simple loincloths, some even naked, working on the roads, if they could be called roads. Naked children played or lounged around everywhere. There were no *kalesh*; in fact, no horses, no wheeled carts.

Most of the buildings seemed to be made of mud bricks and were single story. The ones closest to the track looked like both housing and business premises.

There were stalls selling fruit and vegetables or flat breads piled high, fish and the occasional animal carcass. There was a range of colourful spices. The frontage of the buildings was multi-coloured, like the village back on the west bank of Luxor.

Men were sorting fruits and vegetables, others piling up flat breads. Some dressed in white robes and had bald heads, that made them look much like the ancient priests Ed had seen in books about old Egypt.

We passed by one shop where men were having their heads and beards shaved by a small team of barbers, which reminded me of Greece.

It was dusty but otherwise quite clean, although it smelt strongly of sewage.

"And another thing", Ed said aloud, "there's no street lamps or telegraph poles. This is obviously some sort of representation of the way people lived centuries ago but how the fuck we got here and where the fuck we are, I don't know. They are all looking at us; some are even bowing. But nobody is making any noise. What happened to all the kids shouting welcome?"

They could see men constructing more buildings, whilst other buildings seemed occupied by a variety of men doing their tasks.

Men and small boys herded goats; others carried fish hanging from sticks.

The few women that were visible were bare-breasted, which was most unusual in a Muslim country, even in simulations made for tourists.

Ed felt considerably over-dressed in his *djellaba* and me, Myhat, on his head. Hardly anybody wore anything on their heads.

Thinking of *djellabas*, Ed could not help himself thinking of Ana's body beneath hers. He became aware of his thoughts and decided to focus where they were being taken; or at least try to.

Soon they could see the palace just ahead. It was a two-storey building decorated with coloured flags, fronted by large wooden gates with a row of guards dressed in purple tunics and holding spears and shields.

Beyond that Ed could see a large open courtyard with what looked like a pool of water where ducks and geese were settled beneath the surrounding trees. Beyond that, the palace looked exotic and grand. The building looked like it was made out of stone, with stone statues of gods flanking the main entrance, and two more guards standing each side.

The guards with whom Ed and Ana were walking turned off this road, which was looking in better condition here, and walked a short distance towards a two-storey house made out of stone; another two guards stood outside. Our escort spoke to one of them and they allowed him to go inside. Ed and Ana stood near the doorway, surrounded by eight armed guards who said nothing.

It was not long before the first guard returned from within the house, accompanied by a young man who looked about twenty-two years of age, dressed in some sort of ceremonial gown of blue colour, a blue tunic over a short blue kilt, a blue sash across his chest and wearing a dagger at each side, with sandals on his feet; he had long dark hair, braided on one side; he wore a chain that looked like gold around his neck. His hair looked like a wig.

He beckoned Ed and Ana inside and spoke to them in a language that Ed did not recognise, although he knew it was neither Arabic or English. It was a sort of clicking and guttural-sounding language.

Ana turned to Ed and spoke "It's like Berber, but not the same; and it's not Arabic that I know either."

With that the man moved closer. He said in a quieter tone: "you speaking Ingleese?"

"Yes, English," said Ana, "We are visiting here. We come from Luxor. My name is Ana and this is Ed."

"Very good, I speaking little Ingleese from my father. He from place Luxor, which is our language we called *al-Uqsur*. Here now, father is Abamira, he is Master of House and Greeter of Foreigners for Great King; my name is Amira and I welcome to *Waset*. I take you now My Lord and Lady Ana, to meet father."

They stood in quite a large foyer with mats on the stone floor, large water jugs and pottery urns holding a variety of leafy plants. There were wooden stairs going to the upper storey and several wooden doors which were closed. They could see through some open sliding double doors into a courtyard beyond.

They could see a man sitting on what could have been a raised throne, being fanned by a large dark-skinned man dressed only in a loincloth. As they were led towards the courtyard by this Amira, Ed could see that there was running water passing through the courtyard and, in the water, what looked like water lilies and other plants, including rushes.

As they entered the courtyard the man, who looked to be about sixty years-of-age, older than Ed or Ana, stood up and stepped down from his raised chair, which we could now see was not a throne at all. He stepped towards us with his hands reaching out in greeting, saying "Hello I am greeting you good Master and Lady Ana. I offer the respect of Pharaoh and his house, oh wise man. We talk now and I give food and drink. Later we make all ready for his holiness."

"We are very pleased to be here," said Ed, "But surely this is not the house of a Pharaoh; is this some sort of touristy thing? Where are we?"

"This place is *Waset* and this is Palace of *Kheperkare Senwoset, Ka of Ra* is created, begat of *Nefertitamen Amenemhat*, Father of *Nubkaure Amenemhat*, Glory be upon his name and his family and those that be amongst his friends; Glory be upon you."

I thought that there are more hats here and wondered if I had any connection with them. Ed did not know this, he was oblivious to the possibility.

"I am Amira called Abamira, father of Amira, First Friend of the King, Greeter of Foreigners, Master of the Spoken Tongues."

This Abamira was a well-fed middle aged man dressed in a purple gown that went from his shoulders to his feet. He wore a bright blue and red sash across his chest and what looked like a heavy gold chain and some sort or medallion. His head and beard were shaved; his face carried heavy blue make-up, mostly around the eyes. He wore heavy-looking gold earrings. His smile was broad and friendly. He did not have many teeth. He wore no hat.

"Now please sit and eat arrival feast. Tomorrow we may meet *Ameny*."

"I wonder who Ameny is," whispered Ana as they sat on small cushions on the floor mats and as naked boys brought in plates laden with grapes, figs, breads, pots that they later saw that contained honey with jugs of what turned out to be a not-unpleasant beer. There were cakes that Ed thought were made from spicy lentils and tasted delicious. Young girls who looked about twelve years old, wearing nothing but tiny loincloths and shining beads, brought water which they poured over the diners' hands and then they all ate with their fingers.

Abamira said he would answer their questions later and was keen to hear their story and how they had travelled. He asked how long they planned to stay.

"Well, if we are welcome, we would stay three or four nights, I think, but we don't have anything to exchange," said Ed.

"Kind and wise Lord, your company and tales will be payment enough. And you will give your seed.

"Tomorrow, after you have been washed and shaved of body hair, you will be ready and fit to have audience with the blessed and Golden are the Souls of *Ra, Nubkaure Amenemhat* the son of the Great God, *Kheperkare, the Ka of Ra is created.*"

Ed looked at Ana, upon hearing that. She simply looked ahead.

Ed asked himself if Abamira was actually telling him he had to fuck some maidens. I knew about the sex acts that some people engaged in and knew that Ed had experienced that himself, although I had never been close enough to feel what he felt or see what he thought about sex.

On those other occasions, I had been either hanging on a hook or inside a box.

I quietly hoped that I would experience more this time, as I knew that sex was not only the way humans reproduced, but often highly pleasurable and pre-occupied much of the subconscious drives of many people.

Ed knew, and he knew that Ana knew, that in the time of ancient Egypt, they had encouraged travellers to impregnate girls chosen for that purpose, to enhance the blood-line. He also knew though, that amongst royalty in those times, there had been much incest. Normally the crown had passed through the wife or sister of the Pharaoh, to another male, which was the reason why many Pharaohs married their mothers or their sisters.

It was not, though, the reason for incest, which was either under the mistaken belief that it would keep the royal bloodline pure, or else it was simply lust.

Not that we are in ancient Egypt, thought Ed but at the same time thinking it was beginning to look like a very realistic simulation or else somewhere completely different to Luxor, which in theory, was no further away than the other side of the hill on the west bank.

Ed excused himself so that he could think about what was happening and asked for the toilet. He was shocked to see what was actually pretty much a working flush toilet. It consisted of a stone seat above a hole in the floor. Above was what looked like a wooden tank of water with a cord attached and when he pulled the cord, the water flushed away the excrement, to wherever it went. Presumably there was some sort of pump mechanism to refill the wooden tank. Maybe something similar to the *Shaduf* mechanism that the ancients had used to divert the Nile and irrigate the fields at the side of the river.

After Ed had returned from the toilet, Abamira started to tell them his own story whilst more beer was poured and consumed.

"Now I will tell how I come here and how I speak Ingleese."

"I came to this place *Waset* from my city *al-Uqsur* or Luxor as they call it in Ingleese, many years ago; now I am 56. Then I was boy 12 years old. I came with my friend after school that day. His name was Kareem.

"That day we saw the brother of my father, who was named Mustafa. My father's name was Ayman."

Ed looked at Ana. She was boggle-eyed and puzzled. She just nodded.

"My uncle was going towards a house on the hill and we knew that nobody lived in that house, so we followed him, Kareem and me, and watched as he entered a hole in the ground.

"We followed him down a rope ladder and into a tunnel. We saw a torch near the entrance so took it with us, along with our school books, which were about the language Ingleese, which is how we were able to carry on with our lessons.

"But my uncle was too far ahead of us and we got lost, in those tunnels. We became frightened as we tried to find our way back. We became hungry and thirsty and tired, and then the battery in the torch started to fade.

"Kareem had one lighter from Cairo. I remember it had a picture of the pyramids on it. We used that until that too was no good for us. Then we sat in darkness, huddled together crying.

"But it was not dark! We could see light above a big stone and we climbed up onto it and then saw the way out. That is how we come to be here.

"But we did not know the way back. We had to stay.

"And you say that was over forty years ago when you were just twelve?" asked Ed.

"Yes." said Abamira, "Soon after I arrived with Kareem we saw my uncle again. He told us we would stay with his wife in a house just outside of *Waset* but that it was impossible for us to go back to Luxor. He told us we must learn the local language and to speak Ingleese and Arabic. Uncle Mustafa had been a teacher of Ingleese in Cairo and used to come and visit and bring us books written in Ingleese or Arabic. Later I started to teach the languages to some of his children and his friends. I taught the tongues to *Ameny* and I still do that today."

"Do you still see your Uncle Mustafa?" asked Ed.

"No My Lord, I have not seen him for about thirty years.

"When I was seventeen, Mustafa arranged that I marry to daughter of the Pharaoh, which I did, the Great Lady Titi-atum whom I grieve for, she gave me three sons and two daughters.

"My youngest son is Amira who is now of thirty years and married with two sons and one daughter.

"My other sons I named after my father and brothers in Luxor. My first son I called Ay-Min-Ra; my middle son is Omar-Min-Ra who will marry *Nefru-Ptah*, sister to the boy god *Ameny*.

"After that, Kareem became a Royal Soldier and my uncle took Kareem to the North to marry a princess from another land and he became very rich. I have not seen Mustafa or Kareem for those thirty years since. I have had no word from my uncle.

"I received news that Kareem's wife, after giving him two daughters, was taken at her will as a mistress by another man from a far off land.

"I was told that the wife of Kareem and the stranger were both killed in a big fire and Kareem took another wife, the daughter of a local merchant and became very rich himself, a huge wealth and a private army. I have not seen him for many years and now he is old man like myself.

"My uncle Mustafa was as old as my own father, Ayman, or similar age and would now be about eighty years old and I believe he is dead. Yet I hear nothing.

"I am happy here.

"When I was twenty-five years of age, I was already here for more than twelve years in the reign of the great king, *Senwosret,,* The *Ka* of *Ra* is created, Master of All Kingdoms North and South, husband of Great Lady *Neferu,* that I was made Friend of the King and given this house.

"Later I was by God appointed as Greeter of Foreigners and Master of Tongues.

"I was there when Ameny, Lord and Prince of *Waset* and all the Lands, *Nubkare,* Golden are the Sons of *Ra,* was brought into this world. As the future Pharaoh grew, I talk to him the tongues of Ingleese and Arabic.

"Ameny has three sisters, and first is *Nefru-Ptah* who is pledged to marry my second son, Omar-Min-Ra.

"We have not had visitors from Luxor since many years and we welcome you. I think Ameny will be very happy to speak Ingleese with you."

"How many people live here?" asked Ana.

Abamira smiled: "Forty thousand are looked upon, by the grace of *Atum* and the Goddess *Waset,*" he said.

Abamira clapped his hands and a boy brought a long pipe into the room: it looked to Ed like an Opium pipe.

Sure enough it was, and as the boy placed a small black sticky lump at one end, ready to apply a flame from a small burning twig, Abamira motioned Ed to smoke.

Ed smoked one pipe, inhaling deeply. It was just enough to make him relax.

As darkness fell outside, Ed could see through the unshuttered windows and lamps were being lit. Abamira told the two travellers that he would get a boy to show them to their quarters. He said that they should stay within the building and should ask the boy servant for anything they wanted. He said that they would be brought beer and food and clean clothing. The next morning they would eat well and then go to be prepared for meeting The Young Lord.

"Mighty Night," said Abamira.

The room that they were shown to was quite small, There was both a large raised bed and two smaller ones. They saw mattresses stuffed with straw and cushions that felt like feathers. Each bed was covered with a large sheet.

Around the rooms were statues of birds and animals. The boy lit three lamps. He indicated to outside the door and said "I am here, you want, you call."

The room was very cosy and warm. There was a wash basin off to one side, next to a door that opened on a commode, which Ed went to use almost immediately.

After that I knew nothing of what happened or did not happen, except that when Ed put me back on his head in the morning after he had eaten breakfast, he felt good.

The morning passed slowly with the couple chatting in whispers, trying to understand what was happening to them.

They agreed that what they were experiencing was real, not a dream but how could people go back and forth in time. That was for fiction.

SEX AMONGST THE ANCIENTS

 It was early afternoon before Abamira came to them.

"Please you like to smoke of the milk of poppy? Then to bathe and we go to welcome celebration feat and meet the First Prince, *Ameny*."

Ed did not relish the thought of smoking a lot of opium here. Yet he knew that it would not put him to sleep so, sure enough, he accepted the pipe again, putting it between his fingers so that his lips touched only his hands, and took in a deep draw of opium smoke.

Back in 1972, as Ed and I both knew, Al, my previous head, had caught infectious hepatitis and was very ill for many months, probably from sharing an opium pipe, or cannabis joints, in Kabul in Afghanistan, a friendly and fascinating country that lacked hygiene and was the host to thousands of drug-taking travellers who had been blamed for bringing the illness to that country.

Ed did not want to risk illness. I had been with Al at that time. I knew how opium smoke felt: not unpleasant but dream-like.

So I was glad that Ed now smoked through his hands.

As he blew out the smoke, I felt him relax. The opium took effect quickly. The boy filled another pipe and Ed sucked upon it again.

The pipe was not offered to Ana.

Instead it was passed to Abamira who put his lips directly on to the wooden mouthpiece and sucked. He smoked three pipes and it was passed back to Ed who smoked a third.

Ed's world became pleasantly hazy as he and Ana were led each by hand by two middle-aged ladies wearing flimsy gowns and what were obviously wigs, their faces covered with black and purple make-up.

Ed and Ana were taken through large double doors made of dark brown wood, into a large chamber.

The chamber was filled with wooden chairs and benches, many plants and idols of Gods and Goddesses in alcoves around the walls. Ed recognised some; certainly there was Isis, Ptah, Hathor, Thoth and some he did not know. Several were with a sceptre and feather headdress that he thought was the local goddess *Waset*.

Then he spotted *Min*, the god with the erection, god of fertility.

His mind suddenly became filled with images of Ana.

In the centre of what he now realised was another large courtyard, open to the roof, was a wide and almost circular stone bath into which naked women were pouring steaming water from clay pots. It was late morning and very warm. The sun lit up the courtyard. There was a strong and pleasant smell of flowers, probably incense.

They were greeted by four women who looked like they were in their late teenage years, dressed in flimsy gowns that left nothing to the imagination and wearing what were clearly braided black wigs that made them look even more beautiful, Ed thought, than they would have looked if bald.

The women smiled as they first removed their own clothing, then stepped forward and started to remove the *djellabas*. Ed did not resist. As he watched Ana as she stood there in her pyjamas, the women laughed as they pulled down his boxer shorts. Through his haze he now saw that Ana, as well as all the other women and girls in the room, was totally naked.

The four women encouraged Ed and Ana to step into the warm water, which was deep enough to just cover their knees as they stood. Ed took me off his head and placed me on a table close to the bath; From there I could easily sense what was happening in the bath.

Two women started to wash Ed with soft cloths covered with pleasant perfumes, first washing then pouring.

I thought he was in some sort of dream as he saw that Ana was being washed too; she was not resisting.

As he watched her, inevitably I thought, he felt a stirring and a rising and very soon, as the one woman washed his belly, his penis was hard again. He was too high to feel embarrassed while all the women, as well as Ana, laughed.

"I thought this was going to happen, Ed. Remember back in ancient Egypt they regarded sexual activity as holy and necessary. I think they're going to want you to fuck at least one of them."

"I'd rather be with you. Come over here and come over here!", Ed laughed.

"Later my darling. I love you; I don't own you."

He was going to find this hard to resist, I felt. I certainly hoped that he would do his duty. I wanted to know if it was the same with all women, for Ed.

The woman was now washing his erection, sliding the slippery soapy wet cloth up and down the stiff shaft and around and under his scrotum. He looked at Ana and almost came then and there.

Suddenly he saw that they held long razor-like stone knives.

He panicked slightly, wondering whether he was about to be killed. Maybe he'd been caught out with the boss' wife or sister?

But he relaxed when he saw them gently sitting Ana on a wooden chair in the bathwater, one of them holding her back and the other sat crouched in front of Ana, gently opening her legs to reveal that delicious cherry-blossom pubic hair.

"Oh my God," he thought, "they're going to shave her pubes."

Just then he felt a razor on his own back, and then another on his chest. They were shaving him too. It felt delicious. They shaved his armpits.

Ed did not have a very hairy back, so it was not long before that razor had reached his more hairy buttocks. The front razor-holder had finished with his chest, seemingly spending a considerable time around his nipples, brushing them until they were hard and erect. Then the ladies shaved his legs. She shaved the top of his belly, then she too got him to sit on a low chair in the water. It was not low enough to cover his groin and she helped him lay back into the arms of the other woman as she parted his legs and brushed against his hardened penis. His head was spinning and dreamy in a delightful way. He felt he had no resistance. Here we go again, I thought.

Of course I was no longer on his head. I had been placed on a wooden bench close to the bath. I was close enough though and momentarily I felt almost jealous and found myself wishing that I was the one about to be fucked. Ed, though, did not even know I was a female hat!

As he allowed himself to relax backwards his penis was now standing fully erect and felt huge again. It was pointing to the Gods. He knew that Ana and all the other women, and who knows who else, were watching.

He felt the razor being softly and delightfully moved from the end of his manhood down the shaft slowly towards his scrotum, which she was gently caressing with her other hand which was also holding his hard-on at its base.

She then held Ed's penis by its head, gently massaging around it and tickling him, drumming her fingers on its very end, which sent him into ecstasy. As she started to shave his scrotum, whilst playing so skilfully with his erection, squeezing gently at its base, he thought he would orgasm, then that it was passing, then felt his come ready to spurt out.

Yet he didn't. He just leaned back and relaxed and enjoyed the sensation, until suddenly it changed.

He opened his eyes to see that one of the bath-ladies was now sitting on his erection, with it inside her, lifting herself up and down until he spurted his hot semen inside her. He could not help himself. It was like a rocket taking off, feeling full of power.

He immediately felt guilty and looked at Ana. She had been watching and was now laughing. He thought he would have to apologise and make it up to her later.

For now, his first thought was that he may have made the lady pregnant and that was probably her purpose.

They made no attempt to shave their heads or Ed's beard.

They stepped out of the water, now completely shaven apart from heads, as several ladies brought them each a clean set of clothes to put on.

One carried Ed's leather shoulder bag, which he had forgotten all about.

It contained his and Ana's passports, some Egyptian money, his torch, phone, notebook and several pencils, chalk and the bottle of water.

Ed wondered if anyone had looked inside it or taken anything. He wondered if the items could change this society in any way, if indeed it was not modern on his terms. How dangerous would it be to take things from the future to the past.

He suddenly remembered reading stories of how travellers had unknowingly infected Pygmy tribes with the common cold virus and wiped out thousands of people. He hoped the same would not happen here.

As he looked into the bag he saw that everything seemed to be there except the water bottle.

"Oh my God, the water bottle's not here; somebody has taken it!" he exclaimed to Ana.

They dressed Ana in nothing more than a very fine purple gown that left little to the imagination, placing a garland of flowers round her neck and more flowers as a headdress. Her shaven fanny was not hidden at all by the gown.

He could see her silhouette, every shape of her lovely body, every time she stepped in front of one of the many oil lamps or flaming torches.

Ed was given a blue tunic with a purple sash above a purple kilt that reached half way to his knees, with nothing underneath. It felt good and comfortable and probably looked very grand, but he could not sit down without revealing his privates.

When he told Ana, she laughed. "Serve you right," she chuckled. "They are not shy here are they? If you get another hard-on, they'll all see it", she toyed.

One of the women handed me to Ed and he put me back on to his head. I was well pleased. He may have forgotten the risks of sex with strangers but there he was again now, his head back inside me where it belonged. It was the closest I would get to sex!

AMENY

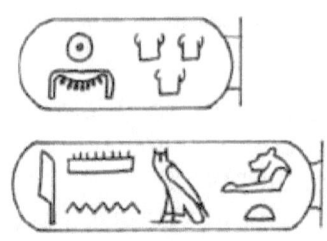

Abamira approached through a doorway followed by two naked young boys, each carrying clay pots.

"Greetings My Lord and Lady, I bring more beer and now rest a while and we will attend the Royal Greeting celebrations and you will meet the Divine Son."

Abamira led them through the door to a smaller chamber that was filled with coloured cushions on top of reed mats on the floor. They lay down side-by-side.

Ed gently pulled Ana towards him and kissed her on the lips.

They lay there chatting and supping beer for an hour or so, questioning where they were. Ed said he was wondering if any of this was real at all; maybe they had been drugged back in Luxor and this was all some sort of dream?

Ana, though, said that it would have to be a strangely shared dream, asking that if it was, was their love making part of it and were they now dreaming that they were discussing a dream, "Inside the dream, sort of," she said.

She said that she favoured the idea that it was all in fact real, not a simulation and that they had come out of the tunnels into history and, based upon the names that Abamira had given them, they were about four thousand years before the time they had left.

She said that she thought that it was certainly possible that Abamira was the son of Ayman, although Ayman had said that Amir was just twelve years old when he disappeared, which was only eleven years ago, which should make him about twenty-three now, yet he looked about fifty-five and had adult children himself. Also there was the story of his uncle, Mustafa, the same name as Ayman's brother, whom they had yet to meet.

"And," she continued, "they speak English! That's pretty weird. I'm half expecting to see the time-travelling Doctor Who appear in his TARDIS. Surely time travel's not possible Ed? What if we changed the past? What if we introduced something that they copied, like your hat? Or if one of those prostitutes got pregnant by you, which I think was the idea. Certainly in ancient Egypt they used to do that. Or if we make them ill, or cause a death, or slip up and tell them the future? I know a little about this time, it was part of my course, *Mentuhotep* and *Amenemhat* the first and second, and *Senusret*. *Senusret* the first was supposed to be the son of *Amenemhat* the first and *Senusret's* son would become *Amenemhat* the second. I think they co-ruled for some time."

"Yes,", said Ed, "and that was after *Mentuhotep*, twelfth dynasty I think. He was the Pharaoh that fought a war that lasted fifty years and eventually he united the red and white crowns and brought together the local *nomes* to make *Waset* the capital. *Amenemhat* the first moved the capital to a place called *Itjtawy*, in the North, what we call the *Fayoum."*

Ana responded enthusiastically: "If that's all true and that is where and when we are now, then there should be the finished Mortuary Temple of *Mentuhotep* on the West bank at *Deir el Bahari*, but no Temple of *Hatshepsut*. I know she was supposed to have built hers alongside and in front of *Mentuhotep's* which was in ruins by her time."

"I did see what looked like a temple," said Ed, "from the boat, when I looked back towards where *Hatshepsut's* Temple should be, but it wasn't as we know it."

Anna continued: "Yes. Maybe we'll get a chance to take a look tomorrow. I think we should stay tonight and tomorrow night and maybe head back to the tunnels the next day so we can get inside when it's dark and we won't be seen. We don't want anyone from here following us. And we should try to find out more about that Mustafa chap and Ahamira's old school friend, I wonder where he is now?"

Ed agreed.

So we would ask some questions and find out what was going on, being careful not to reveal the future or change anything. It was a mystery.

Actually, I thought, it was a mystery I could easily solve, if only *Abamira* or somebody would put me on his head. Another problem for me was how I could communicate with Ed. He was hardly receptive to my messages; always thinking that they are just his own thoughts in his own head. Well, I ask you the reader, who is the clever one? Who is the one that remembers most?

The hour of whispering and hugging and kissing passed quickly and *Abamira* reappeared beckoning them to follow him.

"You must address the God as 'My Lord' or 'Divine Son' You must bow on one knee before him, with lowered head. You must not look directly at him unless he speaks directly to you, in which case you must smile always and answer all his questions. You must not tell untruths or insult him in any way, or his Divine Father the Pharaoh or his family, on risk of death, you must not approach, you must stay on the lower level unless he calls you forward. You are fortunate that now *Ameny* my Lord speaks your tongue, Ingleese."

"Can I ask how old he is?" said Ana.

"He is now nine years of age," answered *Abamira*.

"I hope those women in the bathing pool were not his relatives!" said Ed.

"They are his sisters." said Abamira, "by lesser wives to the Great God *Kheperkare Senwosret*. They did their duty."

Abamira led them out through another large wooden door now held open by a guard. Beyond the door stood four more guards, dressed in kilts with sashes across their naked chests, carrying swords, daggers and spears. Two took up the lead and two followed behind, as they walked down corridors decorated with wall paintings of Gods and

Goddesses on one side and paintings of scenes of workers with crops, fishermen, animals being led by boys, servant-girls with plates of food, soldiers and priests and what looked like bakers and brewers with flat loaves and barrels before them. Towards the very end were paintings of builders who looked like they were raising large pylons and obelisks. It was very colourful and seemed to show many aspects of local life. There was even a painting of a woman helping another give birth, or so it seemed to Ed. Then at the end, scenes of men carrying what looked like mummy-wrapped bodies on stretchers.

They exited into a very large grassy courtyard, rectangular in shape, with a tall circular structure ahead of them. Ed noticed many guards armed with spears high on the walls. Ahead he could see that the circular area had wooden structures at angles similar to the pyramids covered with fabrics bringing cover from harsh sun or maybe rain and probably keeping the whole inside warmer at night. Where they were standing, there was no roof, and Ed and Ana looked up to see a blue cloudless sky.

"I'd like to try to draw some constellations later when it gets dark," he said softly so only Ana could hear (and myself of course, but Ed did not know that!), "because if we are back in time, they will look different over four thousand years … and another thing … those supports for the roof look to be at just about the right angle for a pyramid and that made we think that even four thousand years ago the Great Pyramid would have been hundreds of years old and known about. I will ask about them later. Now I'm thinking I'd like it if we stayed longer, or if we get back to Luxor, come back again. Maybe we could get a trip down the Nile to Giza?"

"Yes and a few other things I bet, like sex and drugs and beer and food!" she laughed. "But I reckon we should go back to Luxor first and get some more information and see what Ayman says about his brother and what we've found out. Funny that *Abamira* is about the same age as Ayman though, and *Abamira*'s sons about the same age as Ayman's.

"Happy?" she said.

"Very happy but knackered."

"No I mean *Hapi*, the God of the Nile. Remember how that chap in the field pointed to the river and said '*Hapi*'?"

"Wow, I forgot about that!" said Ed.

Ed, Ana and Myhat, Happy with *Hapi* on the Nile, I chuckled to myself. I knew how English people often played with words.

Ed and Ana looked around. There were bright oil lamps everywhere. There were two tiers of seats, on both sides with stone statues of the Gods and Goddesses. He did not recognise them all, but could see *Ptah*, *Osiris*, *Isis*, *Horus*, *Hathor* the cow-headed Goddess, *Min* as usual with an erect phallus, *Thoth* the scribe, *Sobek* the crocodile, *Sekhmet* the lioness and the war-god Montu; he spotted several statues of what he now knew was the local Goddess *Waset* with her sceptre and feathered headdress.

The width of this courtyard was almost a hundred yards, he guessed, and about fifty yards in front the area where the covered roof started.

Abamira led them towards it, quietly reminding them not to move towards the God unless he beckoned them, not to look at him unless he spoke to them and not to speak unless spoken too. He told them that they would be served with food and drink, beer or wine as they preferred, and when the God arrived he would take his seat and the celebration would begin. Abamira said that he would call them forward and present them to the God. He said that thought *Ameny* would like them.

Ed could see now that on each side within the area covered by the pyramid roof, there were two tiers of seats, almost all filled by people in a variety of dress and undress. Most of the women were bare-breasted and wore black wigs; the men's heads were all shaven; men and women wore dark make-up around their eyes and some had very bright red lipstick.

There were several palm trees and flowering bushes in this area too. It smelt very heavily of incense, lots of it.

Directly ahead were two tiers filled with what may well have been courtiers or minor royalty.

There must have been seats for three to four hundred people.

Abamira pointed to two women sitting off to one side and said "Young God's half-sisters who washed you." Ed would never have recognised them, from this angle.

Above that was an empty tier apart from the guards who stood each side, as they did on each tier, and above that a large golden throne piled high with cushions. That was also well-guarded. Each side of the throne was a large and beautiful wall hanging. There were large vases of flowers around the throne.

To either side of the throne, on the same level, stood two very large Negroes; one looked as if he was holding a large fan and the other stood by a row of earthenware pots and dishes on a low table.

Abamira led them to two sets of beautiful cushions on the lower level off to the right, pointing out where he himself was to be sitting, on the third tier. He told them they could sit or stand, but should be on one knee and bow as the Divine Son of God entered.

Abamira introduced them to some of the courtiers as they entered, both men and women. This included men whom he said were *viziers*, masters of constructions, astrologers, heads of army and of sailors, keepers of records of stock, of weapons, of history and a whole group of the royal household. Most were dressed in robes and names included the Vizier *Khnumhotep*, and Vizier *Antef*, Master of Divine Construction *Interfikuer*, Lady *Nefertitanen*, Master of Ships *Aker*, master of Cattle *Hanaf*, the Ladies *Fent Ankhet*, *Input* and *Zara*, There was a savage looking priest called *Ptah-em-hebi*. What a good memory I have!

There was an air of expectation and the crowds murmured as Ed and Ana were shown to their places and sat down.

A group of musicians came forward with drums and flutes and harps and other instruments that Ed did not recognise. They started playing a very soft and relaxing tune.

It wasn't long before this supposed boy god walked from behind the beautiful hangings and took his place on his throne. Everybody stood up and then bowed down. Ed kept his eyes on Abamira, waiting for some sort of signal that he had forgotten to arrange. Abamira soon made movements with his hand, and everyone except the already-standing guards stood up.

Well, sensible or stupid, whilst people settled down again and the music continued to play, rising in tempo, Ed could not resist a tiny peek. What he saw was simply astounding.

There sat this young boy, wearing a large hat showing the colours of red and white Egypt, dressed in gold and blue, complete with a large gold medallion that looked almost too big for him to carry. He wore an obviously false golden beard.

Behind the boy there was a large mirror that reflected so much light that the boy looked as if he was surrounded by a silver aura. He had a broad smile on his face. He seemed to looking directly at Ed and Ana, and Ed quickly looked away and downwards again.

As the music stopped, the boy, *Ameny*, Son of God as they said, spoke down to Abamira. Abamira promptly stood up and motioned Ed and Ana to stand up.

"Step forward six paces!" he said to them.

They did so.

Abamira turned towards the boy and bowed; he spoke loudly first in what was presumably the local tongue (Ed recognised his own name) and then in English.

"Oh great and wondrous Son of God, *Nubakre*, Golden are the Souls of *Ra*, Protector of the Red and White lands and the peoples of *Waset* and all the territories of the Great King and all that is Holy and Good, oh innocent and wise teacher of all, for your great pleasure I bring to you tonight, two travellers from afar, speakers of Ingleese, washed and prepared, humbled by your magnificence, the Wise One and his Lady consort, the Goddess Ana."

Abamira bowed again and stood awaiting response.

"Welcome to *Waset,* welcome to God's house. I am pleased to meet you." said the boy in excellent English.

Ed took this as his chance to get a good look at this rich and powerful boy and his regalia. He understood now that he was worshipped as a god.

Ed looked at the boy, then bowed to one knee again and looked up.

"My Lord, I and my Lady Ana are very pleased to be here in your divine presence," he said, "and we hope to serve you well during this brief time of what we hope will be the first of many visits."

"Step forward and approach."

Ed and Ana stepped up to the level beneath *Ameny* and stood below and before the boy that was said to be a god. Ed suddenly realised that what was hanging from a chain around the boy's neck looked very much like a clock.

The boy leaned forward and spoke softly:

"I have much to talk about and, as you are from the distant land of Luxor and the world beyond, I have many questions; I wish to speak of the big birds that fly and carry hundreds and thousands of men and women through the sky to far away places, of the power of *Amon-Ra* that runs beneath the good earth and so men are able to use the will of gods to grind their wheat and carry their crops, light their streets and houses and send messages through the air. I want to know about the boxes of pictures that move with spoken word and music and are in the homes of every man. I want to know about the creatures that are called, in that place, horses and pull carriages through the streets. And the big boats said to be bigger than the Most Royal Barges of the King and carry people along the Great River *Hapi*.

"First though, we have fun and drink. Tomorrow we will speak together."

Music was playing again and dancing girls, wearing different coloured and loose fitting almost translucent gowns with their black wigs covered with flowers, began to move their bodies to the sounds, gathering speed so that their gowns whirled in the air around them. Jugglers entered the arena, throwing daggers and spears high into the air and catching them as they did their acrobatics: some juggled with flaming torches.

Ed became concerned in case a sharp spear or even a fire-stick was ill-thrown and hit one of the dancers.

Ed was drinking beer fast and his cup was being filled often.

He found the dance stimulating and imagined Ana as a dancer too; one dancer did in fact look much like her. She had a nice body, he could see. Ana was happily sitting next to him, quite close and warm so that he could smell her own perfume above even the smell of the incense. She was swaying to the music and also drinking beer. He hoped he would not get an erection right now. In this kilt everyone would see. It was difficult enough keeping his manhood out of sight. Not that anyone seemed bothered. There were plenty of bare chests on display and genitals too and, as he looked around, he saw that several spectators seemed to be proudly displaying their erections.

As the dance continued, another group joined in from the sides.

These all had painted faces or wore masks. They had much shorter dresses; in fact above the knee. They seemed much more clumsy than the other girls. The girls moved aside so that the new dancers had more space. *Ameny* was laughing loudly and clapping his hands.

As the new girls swirled around, their short dresses were swirling in the air around them. Ed looked closer. He was sure some of the 'girls; had penises.

The dancing seemed to get worse and they started to bump into each other; one or two fell over, naked arses pointing at the roof. A couple started to push each other and wave their arms in the air. *Ameny* and the whole crowd were now roaring with laughter. Some of the dancers started to pull at each others garments, tearing them as they fell to the ground, revealing the nudity that was underneath.

Yes, for sure, Ed could see now, some were men and some were women. Closest to them he could now see a dwarf with a huge erection; it must have been a foot long. Several naked women started dancing around him, rubbing their bodies against his. Suddenly one girl jumped on to him; he clasped her as she seemed to slide onto his erection and he started to perform a very strangely funny gyrating movement, much exaggerating the sexual act. She threw her head back into the air and jumped off, the erection was still bouncing along.

Ameny was laughing so hard that he was spilling his beer. Ed thought that at nine years of age, maybe he should not drink much beer.

Ed looked at the audience. They were obviously getting quite drunk, jumping about, clapping their hands, laughing and shouting. It looked like a chaotic orgy.

Men and women were in various states of undress, touching each other in sexual ways.

Several men were masturbating quite openly. He spotted some men openly having blow jobs given by the women next to them or in the tier below. Others were having sex in various positions.

Quite clearly, public sex and nudity were not illegal here: in fact they seemed to be encouraged. Briefly Ed thought he should ask Ana but in fact he felt no stirring in his own manhood at all. It was out of the question. In any case, he thought, I couldn't ask her now in a public arena. That he had wanted Ana in the bath when he was high on booze and opium was one thing; but he loved her too much to ask for a blow job in clear view of a nine-year-old boy, even if the boy thought it all so funny.

This scene continued for a couple of hours: music, dancers, jugglers, acrobats, weight-lifters with trials of strength that looked like Sumo wrestling; at one point several lions were brought in to perform tricks, jumping over people, standing up and rolling on the ground; there were more open sexual acts with various combinations of men and women; at one time there was a circle of men with erections seemingly penetrating the behinds of the man in front as the circle moved.

I knew that Ed found that quite distasteful, but again everyone was laughing or else busy with their own or somebody else's genitals. Men in the audience were clearly engaging in mutual masturbation too. Not Abamira though, or the other Royal Guests close to the boy and not the boy himself.

Abamira was smoking opium. For some reason Ed thought of the value of *Pi*, the ratio of the circumference of a circle to its diameter. Then he wondered why he thought that.

Suddenly, without word or gesture, *Ameny* stood up and walked to the side, exiting behind the long curtain.

The music stopped. The dancing stopped. The sex stopped. Everyone starting moaning or crying loudly, some shouting. Obviously what they are meant to do when the Son of God walks away, thought Ed.

The arena started to empty rapidly, people leaving through a variety of doors.

It was not long before Abamira approached them, telling them once again, to follow. He told them it was time to sleep and he would show them to their beds. That meant going back down the corridors through which they has passed, into what Ed thought must be Abamira's private house.

He led them to a large room filled with flowers, decorated clay pots, small statues of various gods and goddesses, and several raised beds covered with soft cushions. He said "Mighty night" and left.

Ed headed for one of the beds and Ana joined him.

"Ha!" laughed Ed, "He said Mighty Night! Let's hope it is!"

Ayman used to say Mighty Night too," said Ana. "Do you think that suggests recent contact?

ANA

Ed wondered now whether Ana would let him make love to her.

He had known her a long time and they cared for each other, shared a lot and loved each other's company. Yet there had never been any sexual contact between them.

As Ana spoke softly next to him about the plans for the next day, all Ed could think about was her body: he knew that she was quite slender and included firm breasts and buttocks. With that, he felt a stirring in his loins as his penis started to rise and stiffen. He adjusted his position.

I was enjoying this sensation too: if I was right, it may lead to sex. How would he communicate this to Ana? He wanted to smell her. Would he just ask her? Would he pull out his penis and show her?

I was fascinated. Best of all, I was still on his head!

As he drifted in and out of this sexually-arousing daydream, Ana suddenly turned towards him, moving closer.

"Ed," she said, "Kiss me, I want you to kiss me; we've never had more than a peck for decades!"

He reacted immediately, turning towards her, pulling her gently towards him so they were pressing bodies together, he held her head gently and kissed her full on the lips.

That felt good, to me too: I never knew about kissing like this. It was as if they were exploring each other's mouths with their tongues, brushing lips against lips.

Ed felt his stiff manhood, and could not stop himself pushing it against her belly.

Ana moved suddenly away and he did the same. She looked him straight in his eyes: he was about to say sorry but before he could, she said: "Make love to me now."

"Are you sure? It's not just the drink? I really want to if you do too."

"Yes, yes, make love to me, kiss me all over. I've wanted to know you like this for years. Don't worry, Ed, I won't be getting pregnant."

So Ed moved closer again. They kissed and started to undress each other gently. He kissed her neck and then her breasts as her nipples now stood erect. He didn't even care if anyone saw them.

Whilst Ana kissed him on his lips, she had slid down and took hold of his manhood.

I was just laying there close to the mat on the floor, but close enough to see what Ed saw, those wonderful breasts glistening in the moonlight. That beautiful shaven place. Those wonderful eyes reflecting the light. I could smell and taste as he did; best of all I could hear his thoughts, feel as he felt.

Ed thought he had never been so hard.

Ana was making sexy little murmurs as Ed's breathed slower and then faster. He felt he was in heaven.

They had sex; they called it fucking. It was the first time that I had felt that. It was certainly very enjoyable for Ed.

"Wow, that was incredible. I came twice," said Ana. "I am so happy."

Ed felt happy too. He pulled Ana closer again, now they were both naked, pulling a sheet over them, concerned in case anyone was watching.

That experience for me was an eye-opener indeed. I'm just a hat after all. Now a jealous hat.

I knew, of course, I could not change that, so I looked forward to being close enough when it happened again, as I knew it would.

For now though, it was over, as Ed was soon asleep in Ana's

arms. She laughed as he snored for a while, then went silent.

I can tell you that Ed felt very happy and pleased with himself when he put me back on his head. Ana seemed to be glowing.

I had been on Ed's head the whole time whilst we were in that arena and it was as new an experience to me as it was, I knew, to him. I wondered what else could happen in this place so different from anything I had ever witnessed before, so very far in time and space from that barber's shop in Thessaloniki in Greece, where I had first met Al almost forty years earlier. I must say now that I was having a wonderful education on our travels. And, I felt, I was becoming more and more fond of Ana.

"Mighty Night, Ed."

The following morning Ed awoke and his first thought was that he had been dreaming the whole previous day, that he was in fact still in Luxor or even Norwich, that he had not had sex with Ana at all, let alone the two in the bath. He turned to see Ana laying naked, still asleep and close to him.

Then he wondered if it was, in fact, real.

He sat on a wooden stool and started to munch on some bread and eggs: the eggs looked as from not just chickens but also ducks. He smelt the beer. He wanted a cup of tea with milk and vowed that if they ever returned he would bring some tea bags, plenty of them.

There was nothing else to drink, so he supped on beer. He did not want to get drunk at this time of day. Ana was already difficult for him to resist and as he thought about her, he could not help it, his penis started to rise again in it's morning glory.

"Did I really fuck her?" he thought and soon decided that in fact he had. It must have been real, he thought, as he felt his shaven crotch. Then he remembered the women in the bath.

Ana got out of bed and stretched her wondrous body in front of the large window.

After they had eaten a small breakfast and taken some small amount of beer, the almost naked children returned and removed the trays, replacing them with plates of sweet cakes. They brought more beer.

After a while Abamira entered through the doorway. Ed and Ana were both dressed again, wearing the fresh costumes that Abamira had give them, with Ed in a pant-less kilt. A boy accompanied him, bringing their *djellabas*, Ana's pyjamas and Ed's boxer shorts. He put them on.

Almost sadly, he watched as Ana took off her transparent gown, put on her pyjamas, then put the gown on top. Ed was a little disappointed when he realised he may not see her body for the rest of the day.

Abamira told them to follow him and explained that the Boy God was taking them to fish on the river and wanted to speak with them. Their every need would be met and their total honesty required. Abamira said that he himself would not be with them but his son Amira would be. He said that both Amira and *Ameny* spoke quite good Ingleese, so they would not have a problem.

They were led back out of the house, by Amira, back down the road and once again accompanied by guards, to see and board a large and colourfully decorated wooden boat, with both sails and oars. They climbed on board.

Quite soon *Ameny* joined them with quite a few, a dozen or so, guards and about the same number of well-dressed men and women, most of whom boarded smaller boats also moored nearby.

Small crowds of local people cheered and clapped as he boarded the boat, also being followed by several young girls that were probably about his own age, all flimsily dressed, one or two with small breasts, maybe a few years older than him.

They all giggled and hid their faces whenever he looked at them or spoke to them. It was strange that they hid their faces and not their bodies. Ed wondered if the future bride was there.

The boat had sails as well as oarsmen, about six on each side.

Ed knew that if *Ameny* was going to ask about planes and electricity and TV sets, it was going to be very hard to explain it. Yet, as *Ameny* already knew about those things, presumably from Abamira, he could not deny their existence. He wondered if he could just say it was magic.

He decided to say that those stories were true but he did not understand how it worked.

They not tell the Royal Boy that they had been on planes many times, or that their lives were almost controlled, in cities at least, by the power known as electricity, which men and women had to pay for.

He said that TV's were boxes powered by electricity and which told stories or news and showed pictures but he did not know how they worked.

Ameny asked if Ed and Ana could bring him a TV next time they came to visit. Ed simply said that it would be very difficult but that a TV would not work here without electricity.

Ameny said that he would ask his *Vizier* to make a box that a man could stand in and a window through which he could announce news or tell stories and show paintings. First, he said, it would be only for the palace but one day maybe all the people could watch them in the streets and markets in the town.

Ed thought of Egyptian 'Punch and Judy' shows and laughed to himself.

It was then that Ed saw that the gold medallion that he had seen hanging from a gold chain around *Ameny's* neck, was, in fact, another timepiece, as he had thought. A functioning watch in this age? He asked *Ameny* politely where he had gotten it from. The boy god replied that it was a gift from his father the Great God and that was able to count the time and show where the sun would be even if it was indoors.

They spent the pleasant morning chatting and laughing together until the heat of the sun became too hot and then they headed ashore. They had hardly moved on the river at all.

Nobody had actually done any fishing, not that Ed saw anyway. Ana had spent most of the time laying in the sun. She kept her clothes on though.

They were escorted back to the house of Abamira where they feasted on fish which he said *Ameny* had "caught that very morning", bread and fruit along with more beer.

There were piles of onions and garlic and green herbs, vegetables that looked a bit like carrots, olives and a bean stew. It was all delicious.

As he started to feel the effects of the beer he wondered if today was to be a repeat of yesterday. In some ways he hoped so, but in others he hoped not: mostly he wanted to be with Ana. Besides the possibility of more sex, they had so much to talk about, so many mysteries to solve.

Also, they had to decide when to leave and whether to take anything back with them? Maybe a small statuette of a god, certainly an oil lamp. He planned to ask Ana to do some sketches. He did not feel happy about taking pictures with his phone and it was not working anyway. He had to keep his phone well-hidden. He did not want to even try to explain what it was.

Ed remembered the water bottle, a sobering thought that

replaced the constantly reoccurring images of the naked Ana in his arms, in his mind.

So this was their third night. In the evening there had been more entertainment in the arena, which they attended with Abamira and Amira, but the boy God was not there. It didn't seem to have the same sort of energy.

Ed and Ana had agreed that they would try to get back to Luxor the following day as they thought that by now people may be asking questions there. They wanted to talk with Ayman again.

So they told Abamira and he said that he would arrange an escort back across the river if they wished, or a boat along the river as far as they needed.

Then they made their farewells and went back to their room.

I know they had sex again that night. It made Ed feel good; that was good enough for me.

The following morning they donned their washed undergarments and djellabas, dressed as they were when they had arrived. They had another good breakfast with fish.

About mid-morning, Abamira entered their chamber. He told them that *Ameny* had asked him to thank them for meeting him and that he hoped that they would return soon and he would take them on his boat along the Nile to visit the ancient pyramids in the North and visit the camp of the Pharaoh.

Amira arrived and asked if they were ready and prepared to cross the river. They would be provided with a Royal Guard to escort them to the edge of the cultured land where they would make their own way.

That is exactly what happened, with no ceremony and no goodbyes. It was another hot day, but now the guards carried some pots and gourds containing beer. Ed had never found the missing plastic water bottle.

Quite soon, late afternoon now, they had climbed the hill towards the hidden boulder which Ed had marked with chalk.

On Ana's suggestion, they did not go straight to the boulder in case they were being watched, but instead decided to sit and wait until the sun went down. Once they knew exactly which boulder to climb, they could enter without being seen. They still had their candles and had also brought a small oil lamp. That and the gourd were the only physical proof of where they thought they may have been, which was four thousand years in the past.

As they sat there chatting about what had happened, they both said that it was all becoming less and less real, yet they had the oil lamp. Ana checked her phone. It still was not working at all.

Once it was dark enough, they quickly found the boulder and climbed through. Ed switched on his torch.

They climbed the other boulder and without delay, followed the chalk marks back through the tunnels. At some points there were other tunnels leading off and Ed said he would one day like to see where they led.

"If we actually went four thousand years into the past, those corridors could lead anywhere," he said.

2010 LUXOR

As they climbed back up the rope ladder at the entrance, Ed saw that it was still dark, as expected. If they had climbed back into the tunnels at about eleven pm and took about forty-five minutes, it was now just before midnight.

"I'll phone Ayman, he may still be awake. Or else we'll have to phone him in the morning. That's if the phones are working."

He took out his phone and switched it on.

"It's working," he said, "but the clock's wrong. It says it's ten past four in the morning. Hang on, the date is wrong as well. According to this it's just the day after we left; in fact less than twenty-four hours.

"I can't phone him now, til we check the time. Let's just walk back to the hotel. It's not far and I don't feel sleepy at all."

As they left the house, Ana mentioned that it was starting to get light. She looked at her own phone and said that said now twenty past four in the morning.   People were in fact starting to wake up. They rapidly walked back to the hotel which was already open, said good morning and collected their keys.

"I'll phone Ayman at nine," said Ed.

That is what they did, first lazing around chatting and planning, then pushing together the two beds, helping each other out of their clothing with plenty of kissing and touching, then, when Ed was standing erect once again, they had sex. I was on the bedside table and was able to share the joy of Ed's orgasm. I wondered if I could ever be on Ana's head and feel what she felt at a time like this.

At just after half past eight, Ed went to the hotel reception and ordered breakfast, orange juice, tea with milk, eggs, toast and butter and jam. At just after nine o'clock, he phoned Ayman, told him that they had important news and Ayman said he would get his son to bring him to the hotel that afternoon and that he would invite Professor Bertie as well.

Ed and Ana had at least a few hours to do nothing, so they decided to do something. They had sex again, Ana suddenly pulling down Ed's boxer shorts which was all he had on, quickly taking hold of Ed's cock and starting to lick the end of it. It did not take long for Ed to react, and before he knew it she was trying to get his whole erection into her mouth.

She's so good at this, he thought, think of England! He came in her mouth. He returned the favour, so to speak, pulling off her pyjamas and panties that she'd dressed in again, putting his head between her opening legs, as she moved herself slowly up and down.

She didn't take long to come either, but that did not stop him. Already his cock was getting hard again. He lay on his back and she moved on top of him and guided him inside her again. She moved herself up and down and round and round on his erection, making pleasant little sounds, until he came again. It seemed this time they both orgasmed at the same time.

Far too soon for Ed, she had removed herself and was looking at her phone.

"It's one o'clock already," she said. "Ayman could be here soon. I'm going to have to shower first. Join me and I'll wash you."

Leaving me on the table, they went into their tiny bathroom and, well, you and I will have to guess the rest.

In fact, it was over another hour until they were dressed again, with Ed having put his jeans on beneath the *djellabah*, when there was a knock on the door. It was the manager telling them that Ayman and Bertie were downstairs and waiting in the guest living room which was equipped, as Ed knew, with comfortable arm chairs.

Sure enough, Bertie and Ayman were seated in the soft chairs. Ed was uncertain where to start with his tale of what Ana and he had seen.

Somehow he had to tell them that it seemed as if they had gone back four thousand years in time, which was not only going to be hard for them or anyone else to believe, but Ed was already doubting it himself, feeling that some sort of trick had been played on them, some sort of hallucination or dream. Yet he had the gourd and lamp and well as shaven genitals to confirm that something strange had indeed occurred.

How was he going to tell Ayman that he had met and talked with his missing son, Amir? How could he possibly explain that Amir had been about the same age as Ayman himself, with sons of his own named after his father and brothers, that he was called Abamira and was a man of considerable power? He was going to have to explain that Abamira had told him that it was forty-four years since he had followed and been left there by his uncle, Mustafa. He would like to meet this Mustafa chap and confront him. It seemed that they had spent four nights back with Abamira but, when they had returned to Luxor, only one night had passed, that eleven years here was forty-four years there, as if time was passing at a faster rate, although it had not seemed like it. He could see that Ana was almost bursting with excitement.

First Ed asked if Ayman had heard from Mustafa.

"No, my friend, my brother is still in Cairo," Ayman said.

At first Ayman smiled when Ed told him that he had found a man who seemed to be the missing Amir. As he continued to explain the age, the sons, the tale of how Mustafa had apparently left Amir and his schoolboy friend somewhere that seemed many years in the past, in the time of the Pharaoh *Senusret* and the future Pharaoh *Amenemhat* the Third, Ayman and Bertie started shaking their heads and laughing.

"What sort of joke is this to give Ayman such hope and then destroy it with nonsense?" asked Bertie. "How can you say you went back in time? What proof do you have?"

Ed showed them the gourd and the oil lamp they had brought back through the tunnels. He did not tell them about the episode in the bath and the shaving of his body hair, and Ana's pubic hair, and he certainly did not want to be undressing to prove that. Actually of course, it proved nothing except somewhere somebody had shaved them. Neither did he tell them about the celebration mass orgy.

Bertie inspected the oil lamp.

"It's certainly nothing like I've ever seen before. I'll take it and get in inspected; and that gourd. If it is genuine Pharonic from the eleventh dynasty, the experts will know, and I will come through the tunnels with you when you go back, if you go back, or go alone.

"Yet it is a good story you tell, worthy of a book or film, so carry on, please."

Ana suddenly started telling them how they had been taken across the river and had armed guards, that some of the people including Amira and Abamira and the future Pharaoh spoke good English.

She told them all about the bathing, the shaving, the orgy and the fishing trip, leaving out only the details of their sex sessions.

During that time they had been drinking tea with sweet cakes.

"I did miss a cup of English tea with milk," said Ed; "all they had to drink was beer and wine."

Mid-afternoon, Ayman phoned Youssef who collected him and Bertie in his taxi and they left with the oil lamp and gourd. "It may take a couple of weeks to study these," he said.

Ed and Ana chatted and agreed that they would wait two weeks and in the meantime they would go by train to Cairo, visit the pyramids and museum and study the periods before the twelfth dynasty to see what was known. They would also ask about Mustafa, maybe even speak with him.

The following day they ordered a taxi and took a train, in such a rush that, unbelievably, Ed left me on the bedside table in the hotel room. I was placed on a hook in the reception area, where I had no choice other than to stay.

I wished and prayed, although I was not sure to whom, that Ed would in fact come back and that I would be on his head again, wherever he went. One again I thought he cared more about Ana than he did about me, yet that was not the first time that he had left me on a hook or put me in a dark box.

I expect that you, the reader, can guess that they did come back, about six days later. They had learned something of the age they had travelled too, although little new information was available. They had found no trace of Mustafa although there were probably many thousands of Mustafas in Cairo.

They visited Ayman several times and together talked about the four of them going back through the tunnels, about what to take and what not to take. Ayman was unsure that he could himself make the journey, due the problems with his legs, and said he might send one of his sons.

At the end of the second week, Bertie called at the hotel and said that the lamp was authentic, "although," he said, "there was no genie when he had rubbed it."

Bertie told them that he had also been to Cairo and contacted several rich business friends, asking about Mustafa. He had discovered that Mustafa was well known in certain circles, often offering expensive artefacts that had origins in the eleventh and twelfth dynasties and owned a very large property in Cairo and several in other countries including the US, Japan and the UK. Mustafa had been selling such items for over a decade and was now a very rich and secretive merchant of antiques.

Bertie said that they should leave no more time as this discovery was to be investigated with urgency, although he had told the story to nobody else. He wanted to leave with just the two of them that very evening, as soon as it was dark.

So that is what we did. First though, they booked out of their little hotel, giving their bags to Youssef to look after, as they intended to be away for some time and did not want people to think they had simply disappeared, gotten lost or killed.

THE RETURNING

We entered, passed through, and exited the tunnels quickly. Bertie was not interested in anything but getting through. As Ed had suggested, all three wore *djellabas*. I gripped firmly on top of Ed's head. Ed made sure the chalk marks were all still visible.

When we came out over the exit boulder, it was daylight.

"Weird! We've only been inside for thirty or forty minutes, surely, now it's light already," said Bertie. In fact the sun was quite high.

"Check your clock on your phone!" said Ana.

Bertie took his phone from beneath his clothing.

"It's not working," he said.

"See, told you so," she laughed.

Ed suggested that they leave everything from what was now the future, except their clothing, hidden inside the tunnel, explaining how the plastic water bottle had been lost and the lighter found. He said that he did not want to contaminate history.

So that is what they did.

They headed straight down to the river where, sure enough, as if he was waiting specially for them, a boatman waved them on board and rowed them across the Nile to where, once again, Amira and several armed guards were waiting to escort them through this part of the town *Waset* to the house of Abamira. He stood at the doorway waiting for them.

"I am very pleased, as will be the God, that you have returned. We thought that you may not return, it has been more than two moons since you left."

Ed introduced Bertie and Abamira.

They feasted and chatted and out came the opium pipe which Abamira, Bertie and Ed took turns smoking.

Abamira said that *Ameny* was about to go by Royal Boat up the Nile towards the camp where his father, the Divine Pharaoh was waiting. That was planned for two days time. Abamira told them that once again they would be bathed and shaved.

Ed was not so keen on that thought even though it started to turn him on, the images of Ana being washed and shaved in front of Bertie. He did not want Bertie fucking her; there would be other women there, he could do what he wanted to them as far as Ed was concerned, but not Ana.

The washing and shaving was actually filled with laughter. It was not long before both Ed and Bertie had erections; in fact it was not long before Bertie was engaged is rapid sex with one of the women, and soon Ed and Ana were also having sex in the pool.

This was certainly an enjoyable traditional reception.

Abamira suddenly appeared. He had been watching all the time. He walked over and picked me up and put me on his head. I was shocked; Abamira was actually a very fearful man, scared of the boy god and his father, the priests and other couriers. Also, then I knew, he had seen his uncle Mustafa far more often and recently than he had said. He told Bertie that his seed was welcome in many ladies of the temple and hoped that they would be fruitful by him.

After they were all washed and shaven again, Abamira led them through the courtyard and corridor to the guest suite, where all three would be sleeping, saying that in a short while they would be taken again to see *Ameny*, this time before the welcome party.

Bertie was grinning from ear to ear. "So it's true then! I didn't expect that. You never told me I could end up being a father here! Who were those women?"

"Relatives of the Pharaoh's son by lesser wives, half-sisters I guess," Ed explained. "I never got the sex, maybe because I was with Ana? I missed out there!"

She pinched him.

Ameny greeted Ed and Ana like old friends, welcoming Bertie too, saying that they would all sail together the very next day, to meet his father, in the North.

At the end of the evening, Abamira took them to their quarters. "Mighty Night," said Abamira.

It was the following morning when they set off early, Abamira having woken the three English people up. It was a much larger boat than they had "been fishing" on and had many oarsmen as well as large sails. This boat was going to move! We were accompanied by about ten other boats, many filled with armed guards. There were also many guards at intervals along the river banks, on both sides. Some were running to keep up with the boats, until others took over.

Abamira was on board another boat along with his son, Amira, and some other members of the Royal Court.

Nefru-Ptah, sister of *Ameny* who was pledged to marry the second son of Amira, Omar-Min-Ra, was on board the royal barge as well as Omar-Min-Ra himself. They were supposed to be betrothed. Yet Bertie became quite besotted with *Nefru-Ptah* and she with him, and they had sex together several times in front of others, unabashed.

Ed thought that may lead to trouble although it was not spoken about to his knowledge. Women here had equal rights as men and it seemed that people could take sexual partners without complications or social gossip.

All the boats were highly decorated with red, white and purple banners and flags. Their boat had food and wine everywhere, so they could just laze around and eat and chat. *Ameny* played many games, such as throwing hoops on to wooden poles held by the guards, and throwing fruit at other fruits balanced on the heads of soldiers, trying to knock off the fruit, supposedly, but laughing loudly when he hit one in the face. The soldiers stood, motionless.

There was also a game that involved throwing sticks and, depending on how the sticks landed, moving wooden pieces like two armies clashing with each other. It was a simple enough game. The boy god won most of the time, until he challenged Ana, saying if she lost she would have to spend the day naked. Ana won that game.

Each evening there were dancers and jugglers and clowns and a lot of sex as young girls and courtiers came on board from the other boats. Bertie, for sure, was having the time of his life. He spent a great deal of the time naked, with a girl or two at his side or sitting on his lap. He certainly was not shy.

Ed and Ana agreed to restrict their sexual activities to the covered sleeping section allocated to them. But they did not restrict the amount of sex that they had. On those occasions, Ed carefully hung me from the wooden struts.

One morning, *Ameny* invited the three English people to see his collection of drawings. There were sketches of pyramids and of gods and goddesses, many of the boy himself, some with his father the Pharaoh, one that the boy said was of his mother. Plenty of animals and plants.

To Ed's surprise, he found himself looking at drawings of planes, helicopters and what looked like astronauts with spaceships, even cars with wheels. He had seen no vehicles with wheels at all, during his visits to this time.

He spoke to Ana and Bertie later about those drawings and they agreed that certainly this could be seen as a corruption of the time-line. Somebody from the future had been here and left those drawings.

Ed wondered if it may have been Abamira's uncle Mustafa, who was not to be seen here and whom, in the future, was supposed to be in Cairo.

A few days later, I had the biggest surprise of life time since I first met Ed.

Suddenly, after playing hoops, *Ameny* asked Ed if he could try me on and if it would be agreeable with Ed to make a similar hat for himself, in the colours white and red, signifying Upper and Lower Egypt.

Ed knew that the white crown of Upper Egypt was officially known as the *Hedjet,* whilst the Red Crown of Lower Egypt was called the *Deshret.* After Egypt had been unified, the double crown, red and white, was called the *Pschent.* That was several hundred years before *Ameny* and the double crown would be worn by him when he became Pharaoh, as it was by his father *Senwosret.*

THROUGH THE EYES OF A GOD

Ed was not in the habit of letting others wear me, although I had been on Ana's head and a few others over the years. He could hardly say no to a boy god who was his host, so he took me off, bowed and presented me to *Ameny.*

What a revelation!

The boy totally believed that he was of divine birth, that he was a god and that he was all powerful. Only his own father was above him in rank.

I realised that that *Ameny* regarded everyone else as inferior, including Ed and Ana, other members of his own family and court, including the many Priests that he regarded with suspicion and as struggling to gain position in his eyes.

He had little genuine respect or care for anyone, not even his own family and, as *Ameny* knew his successors had done, was quite prepared to destroy people's lives and use people for his own purposes.

Ameny knew that one day he may have to dispose of his father. He felt that when he openly worshipped the gods, he was worshipping only what he was.

Ana's name meant Goddess. *Ameny* knew that Ed and Ana came to him from a very far away and mysterious place, a place where huge birds carried people through the skies and people communicated through the air even showing pictures through their mysterious boxes powered by an unseen energy called electricity which was, he had concluded, a great gift from the gods.

Ameny saw himself as indestructible: he could do whatever he wanted to or with whoever he wanted, except he could not fly.

The head of Ameny was nothing like the head of Ed, or Ana,

or any other head that I been upon. The world view was so different that I became almost lost in it.

For the first time in my existence, I understood that it was I that was the superior being. I had a better memory and better understanding of many things than Ed. If I was to remain on the head of *Ameny*, I could rule the world. Ed could never do that. I also knew all about this land that Ed knew of as ancient Egypt. I knew the history and the geography of Egypt, several languages, the magic performed by his *viziers*, the secret ceremonies of the religions, the names of all the gods and goddesses. *Ameny* was descended from conquerors. Life and death were mere illusions for him; he was part of a greater plan.

Maybe I was more limited to where I could travel and what I could do than these human beings but I could experience and remember much more. Although they may not fully realise the truth of it themselves, I could even get my memories written down by whoever wore Myhat; well, that is how it had happened with Al.

Maybe with practice I could learn to use that connection to communicate ideas, even take control of people's decisions without them even knowing.

If I could do that, with *Ameny* when he ruled the kingdoms, I could surely be a goddess.

It was also whilst upon *Ameny's* head, that Ed mentioned that he and Ana wanted to visit the Pyramids. He asked *Ameny* if that was possible and he said that it was. The boy god knew that the pyramids were many thousands of years old, much older than the Egyptology experts and their books had speculated, which would have been a few hundred years before the time we were now in. *Ameny* believed that the pyramids which we knew as Khufu or Cheops, Khafre or Chephren and Menkaure or Mykerenus, as well as the Great Sphinx, had been built by the Gods that once walked these lands, using magic thousands of years earlier.

I understood that several of the previous Pharaohs had

attempted to build their own copies, such as *Djoser* and *Unas*, but none were so godly, so big, so complex or so accurate in their dimensions.

The strange thing was that *Ameny* had never been inside the pyramids, whereas Ed and Ana had entered two, some four thousand years in the future, as tourists.

I must admit, I was almost disappointed when passed back to Ed.

Ameny spent some time telling Ed, Ana and Bertie about the history of his predecessors.

"Our great land was united about one thousand years before now, by a great military leader called *Narmer* who came across the desert. Before him the greatest king was called *Scorpion*. There have been uprisings since then, as well as foreigners coming to try to win Egypt, but they were all defeated.

"Hundreds of years later, some great gods, such as Kings *Djoser* and *Unas*, tried to build copies of the Big Pyramids in the North, which you may see. Those pyramids were built in steps, one on another, but were not as big or complex as the ancient ones.

"Several centuries ago, the Great God-Kings *Khufu*, *Khafre* and *Menkaure*, blessed be their names, had found it impossible to reproduce the Great Pyramids that bear their names, so took the names of the Great Gods that had built them many thousands of years earlier, before the flooding of the land, and claimed the Pyramids as their own.

"It is said that a few hundred years ago *Khufu* opened the greatest of all and sent in workers to explore the inside, telling them to leave their marks to make claim to all the God's that the pyramid was his. He had temples built in his own name, so that the people would worship him as the greatest god of all. Even today the priests run the temples there, allowing only certain people access, claiming them as theirs.

"There was a great drought throughout the whole land when the Great God Hapi abandoned the people and the river dried up, with many people dying;

"The land became filled with strife and wars, between the *nomes* that each wanted power for themselves.

"It was the great warrior *Intef,* son of *Mentuhotep* the first of that name, who overcame rebellion and brought together the nomes. There were three kings with the name *Intef.* But it was the Great God *Mentuhotep*, the second of that name, the son of *Intef* the Third and *Iah*, that brought true unification in the lands, and *Waset* became a great city.

"It was the time when *Waset* was first taken as the Capital City of the Lands of Egypt Upper and Lower.

"War continued until put away with by Divine Pharaoh *Nebhetepre Mentuhotep*, the second of that name who sent our armies North and South, bringing back great knowledge and gifts from Phoenecia, bringing also much wood of the cedar tree from Leban for the building of boats.

"Son of *Nebhetepre* and Big Lady Queen Tem and the third king of the name *Mentuhotep* sent armies to Punt and brought back many treasures.

"His son by Queen *Uni*, the fourth of the name *Mentuhotep*, *Nebtawyre* ruled for only seven years and was succeeded by his Vizier, the Great God Amenemhat *Sehetepibre* and his Great Lady Queen Nefertitamen, my own grandparents, who also built a great pyramid.

"My own father, the greatest king of all history, *Khepekare Senusret*, the first of his name and Lord of all the lands, ended the years of wars and rebellions. He is building his pyramid already, in the North, at I*ty-Tawy*, where he will make his capital city; close to the waters in the desert. That is where I will travel to meet him. That is where one day, I will build my divine pyramid.

"My father is building also a great white temple near *Waset*, in the Holy Place of *Ra-Atum*.

"Having ruled besides my grandfather and taken as his own wife, my Divine Mother, *Neferu*, my father became the Great God himself upon the taking of the Divine Journey to his afterlife, by my grandfather.

"So you see Mister Bertie, Master Ed and Goddess Ana I am descended from the Gods themselves and one day I will sit alongside my Divine Father and then take my own position upon the Divine Throne, become ruler myself of the two lands and beyond. Then I will build my own pyramid, when my father is taken on his journey to become *Ra*.

"Great and Holy am I, though of short years until now, and powerful I will become, putting down the enemies of Egypt and of God and one day men will remember and speak of me, with reverence and prayer, I, *Nubkaure*, the second of the name *Amenemhat*.

"But at this time, you, my friends, may call me *Ameny*."

The boy clapped his hands and food and beer were brought to us.

I was, once again, amazed, that such a god could bear my name as part of his own name, *Amenemhat*.

It was then that, having seen through the eyes of the young god, that I realised that I too was Divinity itself, that my spirit had passed through all time, to be worn on the heads of people great and lesser sorts, and that my destiny was to be upon the head of Ed, known here as the Wise One; how thankful I was. If only Ed knew!

The whole journey from *Waset,* later known as Luxor, to what was to become known as Cairo, was one of over three hundred miles, over five hundred kilometres. It took over two weeks, by Ed's reckoning, but he was unsure.

Finally it was announced that they were approaching the camp of the "Army of God". I wondered if I would ever be on the head of the living God, the Pharaoh that ruled the world.

The boats were moored on both banks of the Nile. Messengers came abroad to announce that The Great God Senwosret was not in the camp. He had gone to the area of *Iunu* the Place of Pillars, known later by the Greek name of *Heliopolis*, the City of the Sun, to inspect the restoration of the Temple of *Ra Amun*, which was some miles North, to inspect the works and the erection of a great obelisk.

Ed knew that little remained of *Heliopolis* in his own time, much of it having been destroyed over the centuries and now laying beneath parts of northern Cairo.

So it was announced that the Royal Party would wait, some staying on the boats and others on land along with the majority of the army guards to await the call from the Pharaoh.

Ed and Ana were keen on visiting the site of the Great Pyramid and Abamira told them that he would arrange a royal guard escort and that they would travel by camel.

Bertie decided to visit some of the nearby settlements and was also offered an escort. He told Ed that he wanted to ask about Mustafa and Kareem, Abamira's uncle and his schoolboy friend.

Ameny's sister, The Princess *Nefru-Ptah* announced that she would accompany Bertie, along with some of her ladies and an armed escort. They would ride donkeys.

Omar-Min-Ra was not to accompany them; he was to stay on board with the boy god and Abamira.

That evening, Ed was taking a short sleep when he was awoken by the sound of Ana shouting loudly. He looked outside and saw Ana towards the middle of the ship, seemingly arguing with Bertie. As he approached he realised that they were both speaking in Arabic, a language that few spoke here, but Ed recognised. He knew that Abamira and

Ameny both understood Arabic, but most people here did not.

As Ed approached, they lowered their voices.

Ana turned to Ed.

"Tell him Ed, please, how stupid he's being. All the women available here, all the times he's fucked and god knows how many babies could come of it, now the idiot has told me he's in love with *Nefru-Ptah* and wants to marry her. He says he'll stay here with her or take her back to Luxor!

"Not only that, but now he just walks up to me with a hard on asking if I want a fuck!

"Damned stupid messing around with a princess already promised to Abamira's son.

"I know it doesn't seem important here who has sex with who and not frowned upon but talking of marriage and taking her back to Luxor is just fucking crazy!

"What if she gets pregnant?"

Ed was shocked. He did tend to agree, although he didn't think it was any of his business what Bertie did, so long as it did not involve danger for himself or Ana.

So he told Bertie that he was just going to say once that he thought it was a stupid thing to let people know about, that it was probably understandable if Bertie had fallen for an Egyptian Princess, but she hardly spoke English or Arabic at all. As for taking her to Luxor, that was beyond reason. He told Bertie to stop putting them all at risk and enjoy himself while he could, but forget about any future with a Pharaoh's daughter who was already promised to another man, a man of some power here.

Bertie just said "Fuck you, both of you, I'll do what I want and you do what you want. If she gets pregnant then the next Pharaoh or the one after Ameny could be my son and he'll be Senwosret the Second, I didn't come here to be told how to behave by you!" and he walked off.

Ed could see that Abamira was within earshot and had

probably heard the whole argument.

Bertie tried to avoid any conversation with Ed and Ana the following day, seemingly spending most of his time naked aboard another boat along with the Princess.

PYRAMIDS

A couple of days later, Ed and Ana found themselves riding camels, accompanied by about fifty soldiers on foot, and the Master of Divine Construction *Interfikuer*, who was to serve as their guide, riding his own camel.

Interfikuer spoke in broken English to them, telling them not to stray from the camps or the guards and to avoid contact with the priests at the site of the pyramids or near the surrounding chapels and temples, as, he said, they did not like foreigners or people that did not share their religious beliefs and could be very dangerous men. They struggled for power, often trying to undermine the wishes of the Pharaoh who was the true God, whilst they mumbled their prayers and curses. They studied not only preparing the dead for the Afterlife, but also often employed the "Servants of Seth", such as deadly spiders, snakes and poisons, to kill those that stood in their way.

"Crazy men," he said.

It was a journey of some miles and they were to spend three days or so, there and back, camping overnight in tents supplied by and for the army, although most of the soldiers slept on the ground when not surrounding the camp on guard. They had plenty of food and beer, including fish and goats meat, which Ed and Ana did not eat, being vegetarians of sorts; there were plenty of different fruits and vegetables and flat breads, figs and dates in abundance.

Ed and Ana decided to wear the gowns, tunics and kilts provided by Abamira, "By the Grace of the God", with their underwear beneath. It was a very hot ride.

The nights spent under the stars were actually quiet, uneventful but beautiful. Although the soldiers drank plenty of beer, there was little noise or partying. Ed and Ana spent a great deal of the darkest hours looking at the stars, looking for familiar constellations and counting shooting stars.

The following day, they set out on their camels at dawn. It was late morning and before the main heat of the day, that Ed and Ana saw for the first time the great pyramids as they were then, gleaming white in the sun, shining golden capstones, no pyramid overshadowing another.

They were mindbogglingly massive, as they could see as they rode towards them, and nearby stood the Sphinx with its human head but without a beard but the head seemed as out of proportion as he remembered it from 1989.

The Sphinx also looked well-weathered, much the same as in 1989.

Ed considered it just as mysterious in its origins as the pyramids at Giza.

In 1989, Ed and Ana had walked around and even been inside the pyramids. That and this were things that I knew Ed would never forget.

As we got even closer, Ed could see white-robed priests and semi-naked construction workers, in the walk-ways and around the temples.

Ed could see that the head of the Sphinx was different from that of 1989; a different face and one with a beard. He realised that it had since been re-carved.

Interfikuer explained to Ed that the structures contained great mathematical secrets such as the divine ratio of the radius and circumference of the circle, which Ed knew as *Pi*, 3.14 and so on, and that they were laid out upon the plain in the formation of the belt of *Osiris* (what we now call Orion's Belt) as seen in the night sky.

As they rode right up to the pyramids on their camels, flying their Royal banners with an armed escort, the bald-headed priests seemed to stay out of the way.

Ed was fascinated and, as he could see, Ana, was too, by

these huge monuments that were far older than the Egyptologists of his own time had claimed. Older by many thousands of years: "Before the flood", he had been told. Plus he had been informed that they had not in fact been built by the Fourth dynasty Pharaohs Khufu and Khafre who had, as he had been told, taken the names of the gods that had the pyramids built after the previous dynasties had failed to reproduce them, claiming the constructions as their own.

"If only we could prove what we are seeing when we get home," Ed shouted to Ana.

They rode around the pyramid and were amazed that it was preserved quite well, if it was indeed so old.

After riding around for a while, they took shelter from the hottest part of the day under large coverings that had been erected over long wooden poles, and ate lunch and drank beer.

Their rest and refreshment completed, they set of for the journey to the camp, where they arrived just after dusk. They stayed that one night and set off back to the royal barge early the next morning, stopping again in the hottest part of the day and arriving before nightfall. Ed felt welcomed by the many lanterns and torches that lit up the boats and the banks on each side. He felt almost as if he was returning to his friends, although he was well aware that they were all tyrants and powerful tyrants at that. He knew that they had power over the living and believed themselves to have power over the dead, as gods.

They feasted that evening and were told that they would be taken to the east bank and given quarters along with Bertie.

It was a small mud-brick house that had been "donated" by a local merchant. It consisted of just one living room with an open fire in the middle, smoke going up and out through a hole in the roof, which was made of wood.

There were comfortable rugs and cushions scattered on the stone floor. All three of them were to sleep there. The only other spaces under the roof being used for storage, or for a basic run-away latrine.

Bertie was already there when they arrived, giving them no time to settle in before he made an announcement.

KAREEM AND MUSTAFA

"I have found Kareem, you remember the boyhood friend of Abamira when he was called Amir in Luxor?

"Well they took me round by donkey to a few settlements and I just asked around: not so many people called Kareem round here.

"I was directed to quite a large house where he lives with his wife and youngest daughter. They had four children, two have died and one has moved south. Kareem remembers Luxor and his own family. He's mid-fifties now, like Abamira.

"Thing is, he told me Mustafa is a bad man, that he forced him to leave his friend in *Waset* and always prevented them from meeting again. And Kareem said he had never been in the army. He said that Mustafa had told him that Amir, his school friend we now know as Abamira, had joined the army and that he, Mustafa, had seen him regularly until about five years ago when he was killed in battle. Somebody is telling lies!

"Mustafa would not take him home or show him how to find the tunnels. So he stayed here and met his wife and worked for Mustafa who brought him gifts of things from Luxor and paid him enough money to support his family well. But our old mate Mustafa, Kareem said, was very very rich. He owned boats that crossed the great seas and owned palaces in other countries, like Lebanon and Greece, as we know it. He has a private army. But he keeps himself away from people and authorities.

"He said Mustafa collects things from these times, like statues and manuscripts, jewellery and even every-day items and things stolen from tombs of the dead. Then he buries them in places that he knows he can get too, back in Luxor in four thousand years time. Then he digs them up and sells them for fortunes.

"He brings things back here through the tunnels. He has

some people doing that, and when it's here, he sells them to the rich and powerful. Stuff like foods and oils, perfumes and paintings, clocks and watches and jewellery. Kareem had a watch that works.

"It sounds like Mustafa's super-rich and enjoying life both here and there, best of both worlds. If I got that right. Kareem did not speak much English, just hello mister sort of thing. I had to speak in Arabic with him. Anyway, it sounds like Mustafa is a nasty piece of work.

"I haven't told Abamira or anyone else yet, though I bet they know I spoke with Kareem. I wanted to tell you two first. We'll tell him tomorrow."

This was big development in this adventure for Ed and he started to wonder again how safe they were. If Mustafa was so rich and so devious, virtually kidnapping and stranding the two boys, one being his own nephew, whilst leaving his own brother in ignorance in Luxor, what would he do to strangers to protect his secrets and his wealth?

Ed was also wondering how Bertie had managed to find Kareem so easily. Was it a mere coincidence that the boats had stopped here and, in the two days we had been away, Bertie had found the man? Or did he have some prior knowledge? Ed was wondering if Bertie knew far more than he was telling.

Ed told Ana and Bertie about his concerns. Ana looked really worried but Bertie said they were safe with so many Royal Guards and friends. They agreed to talk to Abamira the next day, but when they arrived back on board his ship they learned that he had in fact left with the boy god Ameny early in the morning, to see the God Pharaoh at a nearby site where, one day, another pyramid would be built.

So they lounged around most of that day, shading from the sun, eating and drinking, enjoying the river. Bertie chose his favourite woman of the day and spent most of the time laying naked with her, having sex.

That evening they returned to their house.

A local man brought tributes of food from the villagers. As the man left, he laughed and said "Mighty Night!"

There was a variety of chicken dishes and a spicy-smelling dish of goat which smelled delicious but neither Ed nor Ana ate mammals so it was eaten only by Bertie. There were baskets of fresh fruits and vegetables and cooked stews of peas, beans and onions, with delicious spice flavouring. There were flat breads and sweet cakes made from figs and dates and honey. It was all washed down with a good tasty red wine.

It was a feast indeed, yet without dancers or entertainment other than the stars outside, so after good drink, they started to move to where they would sleep. Ana told Bertie that he was to sleep at one end of the room, whilst she and Ed would sleep at the other. She kept all her clothes on and cuddled up tight to Ed.

It was the middle of the night when Ed was awakened by the sound of somebody retching outside their little house. He got up, picked up a lit lamp and went outside. It was Bertie. He was being sick onto the ground. As Ed approached it looked like Bertie was puking up blood. Bertie was groaning and panting, clutching at his abdomen.

What could Ed do? He called Ana. She called a guard and told him to bring a vizier. As they watched, Bertie stopped puking, stopped moaning and stopped moving. Then he fell forwards.

Ed rushed to him, hoping that he would not choke on his own vomit. He turned him over on to his side. Ana moved closer to Bertie too.

She said that they must not allow Bertie to choke. Then she put her hand on Bertie's chest.

"Fuck, he's not breathing!" she said.

She put her finger on Bertie's wrist to find the pulse, then on his neck.

"I can't feel a pulse, nothing."

She picked up a lamp and shone it in Bertie's eyes.

"Fuck it!" she said, "Eyes aren't moving. He's dead!"

It seemed over half an hour before what Ed supposed was some sort of doctor or medicine man dressed in a brown robe and carrying a large leather bag, arrived.

He casually walked over to the body on the ground. Bending down, he looked into Bertie's still open eyes, he took out a metal sheet like a mirror and held it at Bertie's mouth, he listed at his chest and then he grabbed and gave a tug on Bertie's exposed penis.

He looked at Ed and Ana, pointing at Bertie and then the sky, shaking his head.

Then he walked off as casually as he had arrived, saying nothing.

PANIC

"Shit, shit, shit, he's bloody dead. What we going to do?" said Ed.

"I thought they were going to arrest us when they came to take the body away. I wonder what they'll do with it?

"Nothing we can do now til Abamira gets back. I don't even know who is still here that we can speak to. Or if they'll think we killed him. He seemed OK earlier on, ate all that food and drank the wine. Same as we did.

"I hope he's not been poisoned. What the fuck, do you think we'll be OK, we ate the same food and drank the same wine as he did. Maybe he had an allergy to nuts or something?"

Ana looked at Ed. "The only thing I know is that he ate the goat and we didn't. Do you think he was poisoned? Do you think it was meant for all of us?"

"Well I can't see why anyone would want us dead," said Ed.

"I'm freaking out about that Mustafa. I thought it strange that Bertie found Kareem so quickly and wonder if he knew more than he told us. Mustafa may know what Kareem said. Or there's Omar-Min-Ra. He must be upset about Bertie and the princess. It could be anyone with money enough to get poison and get somebody to put it in the food. One thing, if it was only Bertie they were after and knew we did not eat goat, then it's somebody that knows that. Or maybe we're just lucky, you know what I mean?

"It could even be Abamira or a vizier with their own motives. Or the priests, they kill people, maybe they were afraid he'd get the princess or somebody pregnant and upset the dynasty. After all, Bertie did shout about how his son could be a future Pharaoh!."

My own thought was just how useless humans could be at a time like this. For I knew that if I could be on the head of each suspect, I would know the answer; but could I communicate it? Would anyone really bother to try to find out here.

"He's going to have to be buried here," said Ana. "We can't take the body back through to Luxor even if we can get it back to *Waset*. What we going to do when we get back to Luxor?

"We'll have to tell Ayman but how can we tell anyone we've been through a time-tunnel back four thousand years and Bertie got killed? We don't even know if Bertie had a family.

"Well I guess we've got to wait til daylight anyway. Nothing we can do now."

They went back inside the house and lay together whispering. This time I wasn't even close enough to hear what they said.

Daylight came and two soldiers came and led Ed and Ana back towards the boats. They hoped that they were not being arrested.

It turned out to be two more days before Abamira returned to the boat and met with them. *Ameny* was still awaiting the return of the Lord Pharaoh.

It was clear that Abamira knew that Bertie had died. He said that although no poison was found in the food served to the three of them that dreadful evening, it was thought that Bertie had eaten poisoned food. There were no wounds or marks on his body.

Abamira had sent soldiers to the nearby villages to seek out the man that had brought the food and found his body with the throat cut, in his own house.

Ed told Abamira much of what Bertie said he had discovered about Kareem and Uncle Mustafa: that his uncle was in fact a very rich man with several palaces in other lands.

"How is that possible?" asked Abamira. "When I first came here I was twelve years old. My Uncle was about forty years old. That was forty-four years ago. Now I and Kareem, we are both fifty-six years of age. My Uncle Mustafa will be about eighty-six years now. It must be another man called Mustafa."

Ed leaned forwards and said: "I must tell you some

information that will open your eyes to a great secret, known only by Ana and I, Bertie and your own father, Ayman, in Luxor, and a few others in the whole world, know this secret about time.

"It seems like it is possible to move through time. That is how we all came to be here, in this land, in this time.

"And in different times, time itself moves in different ways and in time here, when four days pass, in another time, only one day."

"When you and Kareem followed your uncle through the corridor tunnels connecting tombs beneath your village, you came here, to a new place called *Waset*, you did not come to the same time as you left Luxor, in our year 1999, as we were told by your father Ayman in Luxor in the year 2010.

"Abamira, I swear to you now on all that is Holy for you and for myself, upon my life, it is my belief that we are now living in the twelfth dynasty of Egypt, under Pharaoh Senwosret the First, in our own dating that is four thousand year ago. We have moved four thousand years back in time to be here now.

Abamira laughed: "Why are you telling me this, you crazy? Your companion is poisoned and you say you are as a god from the future? You saying you can tell me what will come to be? Who will be dead and how? Who will be King? You telling me you can go back to Luxor and I can go with you, and my family, or my father can come here? That is a good story for another time, my Lord Ed."

Ed looked shocked: "I have no reason to tell you anything false now. I wanted to tell you before but you see how hard it would have been, even dangerous."

"It could be why Bertie was killed, to protect all that wealth. When he found Kareem and he told him all that stuff about Mustafa. Kereem told Bertie that Kereem had a timepiece. Did he bring it when you both left Luxor, forty-four years ago or did he got it from Mustafa. If Mustafa is bringing things from the future it could effect how the future turns out!

147

"I think Kareem and Mustafa would both have motives for killing Bertie.

"That may be so, my Lord, but there are others that could have reason," said Abamira.

"For there is suspicion cast also upon my own son, Omar-Min-Ra as he was not happy when Mr Bertie spoke about *Nefru-Ptah* bearing a child that would one day be Pharaoh; and Vizier *Interfikuer* himself has reason to protect the line of Senwosret as do the Priests. There may be jealousy amongst many Nobles that watched as Mr Bertie took more than a share of the women that he could, caring nothing for their feelings.

"The Lady Goddess Ana, although she is blessed, was heard arguing loudly with Mr Bertie only two days ago.

"Lord Ed, with respect, there are many suspects in these crimes. From your own mouth you have made me think of others unknown, from this or that age, who may have motive to protect their wealth.

"Indeed I have considered whether yourself and Lady Ana were also intended victims of a poisoner.

"It is not advisable to tell others your tales, my Lord and Lady.

"We must wait. I am sending out many to find this Kareem, and whether he was my friend or not, he will tell us and lead us to this Mustafa and we will know the truth.

"My lord and Lady, with respect, you must stay with us now on this royal boat until we see reports from our investigations into this death and the body of Bertie is made ready for his next voyage."

Ed decided to accept this as it was maybe the safest place in this world at this time, for them at least.

Later they spoke together and agreed that they would try to head back up the Nile to *Waset* and through the tunnels back to Luxor as soon as possible.

"It's right what Abamira said," explained Ed, "there's a lot of possible culprits and people with various motives, whether it's greed or protecting people or jealousy and even protecting the royal blood line, you know how the Pharaohs often married their sisters or mothers to keep it in the family and for sure Omar-Min-Ra would not have been happy. They even suspect us!"

Ana nodded. "Well I agree, let's get home. We don't know what will happened if they get hold of Kareem and Mustafa. There's the weird age differences too. Kareem and Abamira being the same age as Ayman and then how come Mustafa is not so old as Abamira thinks – he must have been going back and for in time for years, smuggling stuff. There could be lots of watches and stuff.

"Bertie was acting a bit crazy like he wanted to screw every woman he saw. He was shouting about fathering a future Pharaoh which must be blasphemy here.

"We'll have to tell Ayman and he may want to come here. We don't know where Mustafa is. Ayman said he was in Cairo.

"If I have my way I'll see those tunnels sealed up this end."

So they waited, six days it took before news came from Abamira that neither Kareem nor Mustafa or the families had been found, although there had been people that knew them. It was believed that they had left Egypt.

If only I, Myhat, could get through to Ed to let me sit on a few heads, I would know the truth. Then all I had to do was communicate it. I didn't think that would happen. Shame that guy had had his throat cut; he could have told us who'd paid him.

RUN AWAY

Ed and Ana told Abamira that they wanted to go back to *Waset* by boat. Ed was surprised that Abamira agreed so quickly. Then he added Abamira to the list of possible suspects, in his (which is my) head.

He told them a boat would leave in two more days and take them and his son Omar-Min-Ra back to *Waset*. It was to be a smaller boat and would travel with two boats of guards, but it would be less comfortable and faster, taking eight to ten days.

Ed and Ana had little to do but laze in the sun and eat and drink until then.

Their moods had changed so much that although they did a lot of huddling together and whispering, there was no sex. Ed was frightened more than I had ever know him to be. It was the first time that I knew fear.

There was no more news, other than that the body of Bertie would be taken back to Waset when it was prepared and it would be placed in a tomb for foreigners.

Sure enough they headed back to Waset by boat two days later, passing many small settlements, farms and waving people.

One day when Ed had left me on the deck, Omar-Min-Ra picked me up and very briefly put me on his head. I sensed hatred. He hated Ameny, he hated the priests, he hated his father and, most of all, he had hated Bertie.

Apart from the journey was uneventful: they reached the city of *Waset and* spent one night in the house of Omar-Min-Ra, which was far less grand than that of Abamira or the palace.

The next morning, before dawn, they arranged to be escorted by guards back across the Nile and towards the entrance to the tunnels in the late evening, so that it would be dark when they reached the entrance to the tunnels. So that is what they did.

They sat a short distance from the boulder and watched the guards walk away before finding the correct boulder and scrambling through the entrance. Ed certainly did not want to be seen doing that. Inside, they looked for the items that they had left there. It was obvious that they had been disturbed, but nothing seemed to be missing as far as Ed could see, although he was not certain about Bertie's stuff. Ed and Ana collected together their own belongings, deciding to leave Bertie's stuff near the bolder.

It did not take them very long to get through the tunnels and to the rope ladder. As Ed climbed up and out through the entrance, once again, I fell off his head, back down the shaft towards Ana.

This time she caught me and placed me upon her own hatless head and climbed up.

That was when I saw through Ana's mind the memories of what had occurred, from her point of view so to speak.

I can tell you I was pleased, surprised and shocked at how she had seen events turn out, what she thought and felt about Ed, about Ayman, Abamira, Omar-Min-Ra, Bertie and Ameny and the whole lifestyle she had witnessed. I can tell you that Ana has her own tales.

Let sleeping dogs lie, I have heard it said.

They agreed to contact Ayman and ask if he could help them seal up the exit to Abamira's time.

"Ed, do you think we'll ever know what really happened, who killed Bertie?" asked Ana.

Ed looked up: "Well I somehow doubt it. I'm not at all keen on going back and I wouldn't advise anyone else to. I'm not sure that their society had any real sense of justice, only tyranny and I think we were just a curiosity for *Ameny* and his crowd. There'll be nothing in the history either. Really we were not important and I bet Bertie's murder was just one of hundreds, let alone natural deaths, accidents and war.

"Abamira seemed to think there's loads of suspects. They

don't exactly have forensics there. I bet they torture suspects and sooner of later one of them will confess, guilty or not. We can't exactly tell the police.

"Now we're back here, it doesn't make much difference who did it, unless it was Mustafa and he'll have to get back here too.

"I'm also worried about him, if he was taking things like watches and who-knows-what back through time.

"I'm going to start looking at the old tomb paintings, see if any of the gods or kings have anything like a watch on their wrist. I bet they do.

"And I bet if they've ever dug one up, they'd keep it secret.

"First thing I want to ask Ayman is if he's seen Mustafa since we left.

"We were gone a good few weeks there. If it was say thirty-six days, I've lost count, it would be just nine days here if its' really four-to-one. Let's get back to the hotel and see if they have a room, then phone Ayman."

So that is what they did.

They managed to rent the same hotel room as before.

They lay together speaking about what to tell Ayman. The whole truth or just part of it? Then they made love again. Then they phoned Ayman and he said he would be at the hotel as soon as possible. He had news for them too.

It turned out that his brother Mustafa had been arrested in Cairo for possession of ancient artefacts.

He had been fined a lot of money and apparently had then gone to Greece.

So, thought Ed, Mustafa may well have been back in time when he was supposed to be in Greece.

They told the tale of what had happened and how Professor Bertie had died.

They told the whole tale, from the moment they had first met

Amira and Abamira, through the feasting and bathing and royal audiences with *Ameny*.

They told him about the orgies and how Bertie had behaved with the Princess and all the other ladies on the boat journey along the Nile.

They told Ayman that they were convinced that time had somehow moved faster there, in the eleven years here since Amir had disappeared with Kareem, forty-four years had passed there, so that back then Amir was fifty-six years of age. He had taken the name Abamira and had a son called Amira, Omar-Min-Ra and Ay -Min-Ra, some of whom already had their own children. They were living the lavish lifestyle of a Friend of the Pharaoh.

They told Ayman how Bertie had gone searching for Kareem and Mustafa and had found Kareem who Bertie had said, told him about Mustafa and his work of sending things through time, and that Ameny had a watch.

"But", they said, "the life of a foreigner was maybe only of diplomatic importance and no efficient proper investigation was possible. There were no fingerprints of forensics four thousand years ago."

They named the suspects: Omar-Min-Ra, the vizier, a jealous admirer, Abamira himself, even the boy god.

They did not mention that they too could have been suspects.

They told Ayman that they had left Bertie's few personal possessions near the exit boulder, hidden.

They said that Bertie's family would have to be told, and the police and British Embassy, but as there was no body and no evidence, what could they say?

They could hardly say they'd been through time or take the police back with them.

Ayman said that he would seek help and something could be done. It was not the first time somebody here had simply disappeared, wandering into the desert, falling into the Nile or getting lost underground.

Ayman seemed to take it calmly although he was looking more and more confused and more and more worried.

"I do not think it would be good for a man to meet his father when they are the same ages but must be so different. I will not go there and I do not want my son to come here.

"And, my friends, I must find out if my brother Mustafa is involved in some way and where he is now.

"What if," he said, "those people all start coming here through the tunnels?

"They'd be like savages to the people here. They could start robbing and killing and taking so much modern stuff back with them."

Ed looked at Ayman straight in the eyes and said: "That's why I think we should seal up the tunnels at the exit boulders. It won't be easy. We tried to hide the way in from that side but we've got to stop people going back and forth willy-nilly if more people from here or their find their way through. I'll go through one more time and wash off the chalk marks that we left.

"Do you think we could safely blow it up? Can you get dynamite? Do you know who can safely use it?"

To Ed's surprise, Ayman agreed. "I lost my son to those fucking tunnels and Kareem, and maybe my brother, all for riches and greed. I think it must be stopped. We can seal up the entrance from this side too, but not with dynamite as it would cause trouble and attract people. I will start making preparations already. There are plenty of explosives in the Valleys. I can get some and I know Youssef has a friend who uses it.

"I will send somebody to clean off chalk marks and bring back Professor Bertie's things. I do not ask you to go again"

So that is what they did.

Later, when they were alone, Ed said to Ana:

"I just thought, what if there are other tunnels through time? They could be anywhere, not just here. There could be one in Cairo or Greece or even London!"

"Even Norwich," laughed Ana. "There's plenty of old tunnels there and almost everywhere. Just think how many cities have had secret tunnels. I know the Vatican did. And the tubes and metros go pretty deep. I remember somebody telling me there was a long tunnel running the length of Britain. Gibraltar is filled with them. There may even be tunnels to the future."

They agreed to leave the 'who-dun-nit' mystery to four thousand years ago, seal up the tunnels and try to find Mustafa.

As their return plane had already flown, Ed and Ana bought tickets for another flight back to London a few days later. They spent those days in Luxor, staying in a hotel on the East Bank, lazing in the sun, making love and discussing what had happened and what to do next.

Two days later they took the long flight back to London and caught the train from London Liverpool Street to Norwich.

After a few days back in Norwich, I sensed more and more uncertainty in Ed about what had happened, He told Ana that he felt he had to tell somebody what had happened.

They decided to seek out Al and to tell him all about their adventure and catastrophe.

Ed also decided he would give me, Myhat, back to Al.

"It's his hat," he told Ana, "it might have brought me mixed blessings. Love and death both," he said.

Ayman had phoned them from Luxor and had said that the tunnels would be closed "for all time." He had not yet found his brother, Mustafa.

And so that is what they assumed.

AL and MYHAT

Al seemed pleased to see Ed and Ana again, after quite a few years.

As they shook hands, Ed took me off his own head and leaned forwards, putting me on Al's head.

"Your hat, I believe, old chap," said Ed.

"Myhat indeed," he replied, laughing.

I knew he was quite pleased to get me back and I was actually quite pleased to know Al again.

The three sat and smoked some pipes of good hashish and Ed and Ana jostled to tell their versions of their exploits in Egypt to Al.

Al listened as they outlined first their trips as tourists in 1989 and 1990, and of their next trip twenty years later.

But as they continued to tell how they had been through time tunnels to a time four thousand years in the past, meeting those people and even a future Pharaoh, Al laughed more and more.

"It's a very good story, a bit like Doctor Who, but he beat you to it; he went back to ancient Egypt too.

"Maybe I'll write it one day," said Al.

I was amazed, shocked, disappointed.

We had been through all that and Professor Bertie had been killed, even though I knew that Ed did not expect to ever find out who did it, yet now the problem was who would believe their stories?

Here was I, Myhat, full of memories and tales of what had actually happened, even those sexual experiences, drugs, travels through space and even time, and yet I feared I would never be able to tell anyone, not even another hat.

That was when I first focussed so hard of getting the idea of writing first the story of my visit to India back in 1972, through Al.

Now I gave him the idea of claiming that his hat, Myhat, wrote the book about 1972. Of course, you know that it was, but Al does not in fact believe it.

Of course it was I, Myhat, that told the story.

It was several years later, again, that Al wrote this book, about my time in modern and ancient Egypt with Ed and Ana.

It was I who told the tale, much better than Ed could have told it himself. I have the memory of a god.

I can tell you my reader, that when he started the tale, Al did not fully know everything that had happened: there were many gaps in what Ed and Ana had said several years ago.

Without me, Al would have never started and would never have finished the tale.

Al did not know all the details of what had happened.

So this book's author is Myhat. Only I know the truth, for it is I that is that I am the God Myhat-Ra

And there was still the mystery of who was behind the murder.

There is only one person that knows the answer, in this time and that. I have been on that head too.

Perhaps that history is best left as a mystery.

Mighty Night for now

AL AND THE UNDEAD

It was a few years after Ed had told Al his story and I had been returned to Al, that Al's interest was awaken by a news story that led him and Ed back to Luxor.

It was an item about the discovery on rock carvings dated from thousands of years ago: they were depictions, it was reported, of a helicopter and a plane!

Al had read: *"The 3,000-year-old hieroglyphs found in Seti The First's temple in Abydos, Egypt, are said to depict nothing less than a helicopter, plane and futuristic aircraft among the usual insects, symbols and snakes."*

So, I take up my tale with the arrival on Ed and Al in Luxor and their meeting with Ayman. Ed and Ayman were just four years older but that meant Abamira would have been sixteen years older, at least in his late sixties and, possibly dead. Ameny would have been twenty-four years old and possibly co-ruling with his father.

Ayman told them that the tunnels had been sealed up.

He also told them that Bertie had "come back from dead."

Ayman was still living in the house of his brother, Mustafa.

We listened as Ayman told us that much suspicion was laid on Mustafa who had not been seen, apparently since Ed's last time in Luxor and before Ed went back to England with Ana. This time, Ana had stayed in the UK after she had had her first child by Ed. Ed explained that he had agreed only to travel as far as Luxor with Al to introduce him to Ayman.

Ayman portrayed a very different picture of what had supposedly happened to Ed, Ana and Professor Bertie in those ancient days in Egypt; quite different and more complete than the impression Ed had given Al.

Ed had told Al, as Ayman had told Ed, that the entrance and exit from the tunnels had ben sealed up.

Now Ayman was telling them that Bertie was not in fact dead!

Bertie had returned to Luxor several weeks after Ed and Ana had left but Bertie had asked Ayman to keep it as a secret for at that time. Bertie had sorted out some of his local affairs through officials. Officially he was still alive, but had gone into hiding, fearful of his life, until the whereabouts of Mustafa had been ascertained.

Ayman made a phone call and it was not long before Bertie turned up at his house where he greeted Ed as if they were long-lost brothers. Ed introduced Al to Bertie.

Bertie told Ed and Al that he had been employed, for over ten years, by an international organisation known as AFAR, the Agency for Artefact Recovery. They had been investigating the activities of Ayman's brother, Mustafa, as he was suspected of illegally selling stolen ancient relics from Egypt, many from over four thousand years ago and had become very rich in the process.

That was why Bertie was so keen to accompany Ed and Ana back through the time tunnels after they had reported finding Ayman's missing son, Amir, known there as Abamira, a successful and rich man living in *Waset*, a town that eventually became Luzor. Abamira, and subsequently his old school friend Kareem, had in turn told Bertie that Mustafa was bad man who had abandoned them there, telling them it was not possible for them to go back to Luxor and had been burying artefacts to be dug up thousands of years later in his own time. Mustafa had also been taking items such as time pieces back from this, our present era, to give and sell in the past, where he had also become rich and powerful.

Bertie also admitted that he had not behaved sensibly in particular regarding his sexual antics with the Princess *Nefru-Ptah* and tried to excuse his behaviour as a result of his consumption of alcohol, opium and cannabis.

That, he admitted, had made him very unpopular and was the possible cause of the attempt on his life by poisoning. Yet, he explained, the attempt on his life was not a solved crime. He suspected Omar-Min-Ra, a son of Abamira, who was promised to wed *Nefru-Ptah* and it was probable that the poisoning was a result of simple jealousy.

However, explained Bertie, he had also uncovered a conspiracy between Mustafa, Abamira and Omar-Min-Ra, at least. They were all profiteering from Mustafa's time-smuggling exploits.

Bertie told them that he remembered being sick and had realised that he had been poisoned. He remembered nothing after that until be woke up back inside the tunnels, in complete darkness, the exit to the old world having been sealed up from the outside. He had been left there along with a small plastic bottle of water and a modern-day torch, so had soon found his way out by following the chalk marks previously left there by Ed and Ana.

Since returning to the present day, AFAR agents had discovered that Mustafa was living in Greece or possibly Romania. They suspected that Mustafa had links to other times in other countries. No attempt, however, had been made to go back the 4000 years to *Waset*. By this time, in those days, several people such as Abamira may have died and Ameny, the "Boy-God" could well be co-ruling with his father, Senusret *Kheperkare*, also known as Senwosret the First. History showed that "Ameny" was to become the great Pharaoh Amenemhat The Second, *Nebkhaure*.

I, Myhat, can tell you gentle reader, that I had been on the head of the man responsible for poisoning Bertie and slitting the throat of the old man who had delivered the poison food. That man was Oman-Min-Ra, a hateful and jealous man, and in fact his main purpose had been to stop the copulating between Bertie and the Princess *Nefru-Ptah*, especially after Bertie had boasted that he could become the father of a future Pharaoh.

I can tell you, because I had been on his head after the poisoning, that Omar-Min-Ra had acted under the full knowledge of his father Abamira, but they both knew that the poison would not kill. It had paralysed Bertie to such an extent that he would seem dead.

I can tell you that I was not keen on the idea of Al trying to go back to those days and put his life at risk whether it was to find helicopter drawings, time pieces of killers.

Bertie had no way of knowing that and I had no way to tell him. I was worried in case he persuaded Al to go back in time with him. As we know, Bertie had left with many people disliking him and maybe fearing him enough to poison him yet with some reason not to simply kill him.

Truth is of course, I would get no say, despite my ability to watch, listen and remember like a God.

It was a very long afternoon spent smoking cannabis with Bertie, Ayman and Ed. Al was exhausted and stoned: his imagination was going wild: he had ideas of joining Bertie in his quest to halt the time-smuggling activities, to find Mustafa and to discover the truth about the ancient rock carvings of planes and helicopters.

Ed, on the other had, was quite insistent that the only place he was going to would be to Norwich to join Ana. He was not prepared to risk his life; he was a father now, Ed said. Ed was not going back to *Waset*.

Glossary

Abamira: son of Ayman, father of Amira.

Amira: Son of Abamira.

Amon-Ra: Supreme Sun God *Anubis*: God of the Dead.

Ameny, Amenemhat II: Son of Senwoset I.

Ayman: Luxor donkey rides and father of Youssef, Omar, Mohammed and Amir.

Ba: Part of Spirit of Person.

Deshret: Red crown of Lower Egypt.

Djellabah: Loose-fitting robe.

Hapi: God of the Nile.

Hathor: Cow-headed goddess.

Hatshepsut: Eighteenth dynasty female pharaoh.

Hedjet: White crown of Upper Egypt.

Horus: God, son of Isis and Osiris

Isis: Goddess sister and consort of Osiris, mother of Horus.

Ka: Part of Spirit of Person.

Kalesh: Horse-drawn carriage in modern Luxor.

Min: Ithyphallic Male God of Fertility.

Montu: Falcon-headed god.

Omar: Son of Ayman.

Omar-Min-Ra: Son of Abamira

Osiris: Father of the Gods (Orion); Underworld and dead.

Pschent: Red and white crown of unified Egypt.

Ra: Sun God.

Saduf: device for lifting water.

Souk: Market.

Stele: A stone tablet bearing an inscription.

Thoth: Scribe God.

Vizier: High-ranking advisor to Pharaoh.

Waset: Goddess of Waset.

Waset: Ancient name prior to Thebes and Luxor.

Approximate Chronology

Approximately 10,500 BC : The original Khufu, Khafre and Menkaure; the building of the Great Pyramids and Sphinx at Giza

3400 – 2980 BC: Narmer (Menes)
2900 – 2750 BC: Sneferu, Khufu, Khafre, Menkaure
2375 – 2345 BC: Unas
2331 – 2287 BC: Pepi I
2278 – 2184 BC: Pepi II
2068 – 2061 BC: Intef III
2061 – 2010 BC: Mentuhotep I Nebhetepre (Reunification)
2010 – 1998 BC: Mentuhotep II Sankhkare
1998 – 1991 BC: Mentuhotep III Nebtawyre
1991 – 1962 BC: Amenemhat I Sehetepibre
1971 – 1926 BC: Senusret I Kheperkare
1929 – 1895 BC: Amenemhat II Nubkhaure
1897 – 1878 BC: Senusret II Khakheperre

1503 – 1498 BC: Thutmosis I Akheperkare
1493 – 1479 BC: Thutmosis II Akheperenre
1479 – 1468 BC: Hatshepsut Maatkare
1479 – 1425 BC: Thutmosis III Menkheper(en)re
1425 – 1398 BC: Amenhotep II Akheperure
1398 – 1388 BC: Thutmosis IV Menkheperure

1332 – 1323 BC: Tutankhamun Nebkheperure

1279 – 1213 BC: Ramesses II Usermaatre Setepenre

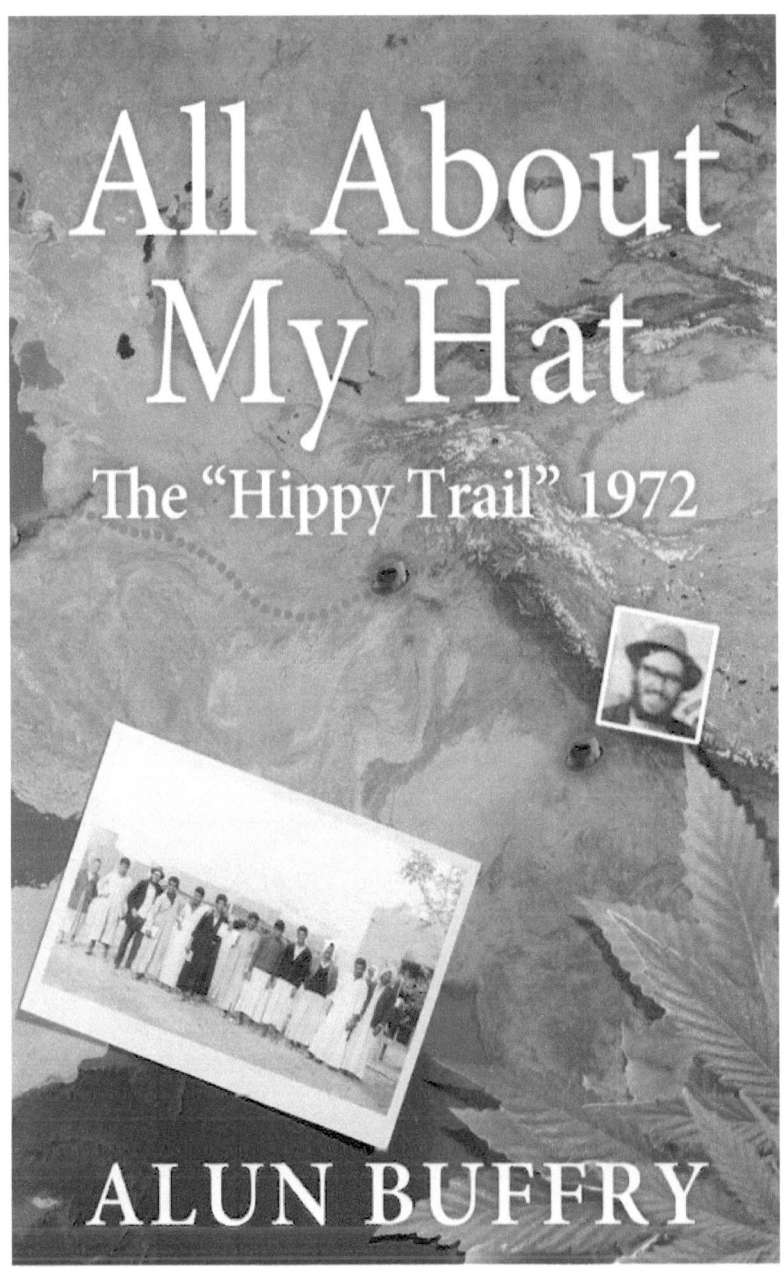

All About My Hat

The "Hippy Trail" 1972

ALUN BUFFRY

ISBN 9780 9932107 0 9

From
DOT
to
CLEOPATRA

Alun Buffry

ANCIENT EGYPT
▲
Up-to-date reference
· *facts, theories and questions*
· *the oldest stories & latest finds*

FRONTIER ▶2000◀ SERIES

ISBN 1 8729140 9 8

TIME FOR
CANNABIS
The Prison Years
1991 to 1995

Alun Buffry

ISBN 9780 9932107 6 1

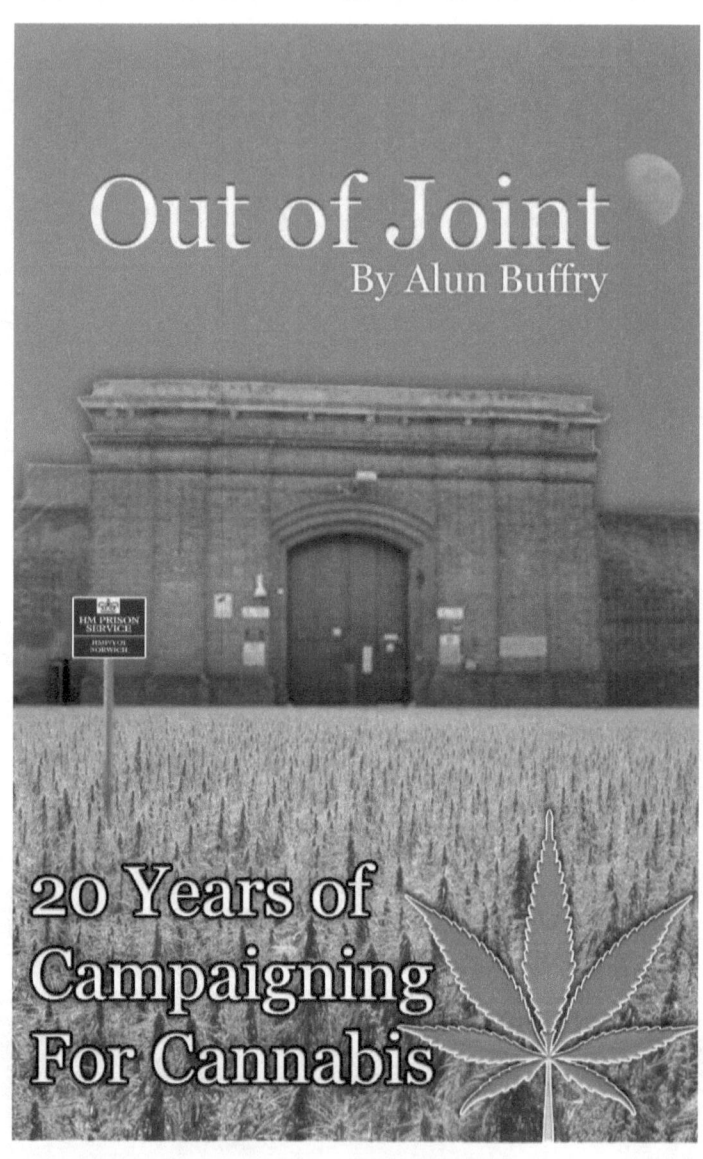

Out of Joint
By Alun Buffry

20 Years of
Campaigning
For Cannabis

ISBN 978 15084202 1 1

ALUN BUFFRY, WILLIAM D HUTCHINSON

Damage and Humanity in Custody

A Comparison of UK
Prison Regimes by Inmates

ISBN 978 15330262 2 4

www.buffry.org.uk/
abefreepublishing.html

www.ingramcontent.com/pod-product-compliance
Lightning Source LLC
Chambersburg PA
CBHW020911180626
46816CB00007BA/2354